The Taciturn Sky

Cinzi Lavin

The Taciturn Sky is a work of fiction. Names, characters, events and incidents are the products of the author's imagination. Any resemblance to actual persons, living or dead, or actual events is purely coincidental.

Cover art: Neyret Freres weaving "Bat l'Eau" *adapted from* "Le cerf sur ses fins" *by Paul Tavernier*

ISBN: 978-1-7366350-0-1

To J.D. Salinger

for writing the best book I ever read

PART ONE

On one side of the fireplace was a French silk tapestry depicting a buck evading capture by crossing a river. Behind him, dogs and a huntsman tracked him in vain. On the other side of the fireplace was a matching work, with the buck having reached his resting place in a thicket in the woods. Other deer were with him and he was at peace.

That these two tapestries, which hung in the cabin owned by Bryce's grandfather, now belonged to him was a realization that evoked wonder. Ever since boyhood, those had been Grandfather's tapestries over Grandfather's hearth. Now they were his.

Also his was a catalogue of property and investments so nettlesome that his family's lawyers and finance managers were still sifting through it. It would be days before the full picture of his inheritance could be presented in detail, but that would give Bryce time to take it all in. He wished he could process all the things he would need to process, and quickly. If only people could die a little at a time, leaving bits of themselves, instead of succumbing all at once.

Woodrow Bryce Parnell's death had been relatively unexpected for an 87-year-old man. He'd seemed well enough until a cough developed and then worsened. He was hospitalized in a timely fashion, but between lung issues and sudden heart complications, the end came quickly. Bryce almost laughed out loud at the funeral remembering something his grandfather had said once: "In the old days, people died in much better health." He had meant they didn't go through the tortures of life-saving treatments, thanks to elaborate equipment designed to sustain life to the point of absurdity. He had mindfully designated himself "DNR"—"Do Not Resuscitate," but it was hardly necessary. Mother Nature finished him off so quickly, Bryce could almost imagine her quipping "Done and dusted," as she evaporated from his bedside.

He was a tough old dog, Bryce reflected. Old-school to the very end, insisting on a three-day wake and a large church funeral; nobody was going to overlook Woodrow Bryce Parnell's death. He wasn't the kind of man that you could overlook. Even in death, he cast a shadow of strength over his empire, his absent influence more pervasive even than in life because it dwelt in the imagination.

2

Two hours later, Bryce pulled his car into the driveway of his sister's house in Tuxedo Park. It had been the house in which their mother was raised. She'd given it to Susan when Susan and Patty married. It was a nice house, with a multicolored stone exterior. The different shades of copper, grey, and brown had a homey effect. Bryce enjoyed going there because it brought back good memories of Mother, and because he liked Patty. She was very personable and helped to take some of the edge off his sister, who could be stern.

Susan had inherited Grandfather's temperament. During their childhood, he'd invested a lot of time with her since she was the eldest, and since her nature was more like his own than Bryce's.

Bryce had been dreamy and lighthearted as a child; meanwhile, Susan and Grandfather discussed things like controlling interest.

Bryce rang the doorbell and was let in by Margaret, who took his coat and greeted him.

"How's that son of yours doing at Fordham?" Bryce asked jovially.

"Very well, thank you for asking. John made the dean's list this semester," she replied. Susan was paying half of John's tuition; she used to say things like "Don't coddle servants"—clearly something learnt at Grandfather's knee—but under it all, she had a heart. Margaret was a good egg, but was as stern as Susan, mostly because she'd had a rough life. Margaret's mother, an Irish immigrant, had been in service and Margaret thought she'd escaped that fate when she married a plumber with a small business of his own, but he'd been improperly insured, and when he died young, she was forced into service to support herself and her son. John was studying law now. Bryce realized with a slight chagrin that John would have a better education than he himself did.

Margaret led Bryce to the room where Susan and Patty were awaiting their tea. Margaret insisted on serving tea every day, come hell or high water. It was a pleasant affair, using Mother's inherited china and a few cookies or a quick bread with a bit of fruit. She frequently served carrot cake, because it was Susan's favorite.

The women rose to meet Bryce, Susan giving him a sparce hug. It wasn't so much a hug as simply a lean-in; a gesture of closeness that implied more than it gave. Patty, on the other hand, embraced Bryce warmly and gave him a kiss on the cheek. In many ways, Bryce felt it was she who epitomized the personality of a sister.

Margaret stood at the drawing room doorway giving a look of impatience, the kind a great servant can manage, firmly but unobtrusively, so Bryce sat down and tea was served. Sure enough, there was carrot cake. Susan took the first slice while Bryce and Patty fiddled with their milk and lemon.

"What is Deek up to these days?" Patty asked, referring to one of Bryce's longtime friends. Bryce and Deek had celebrated the Fourth of July at Susan's a few months earlier.

"Oh, the usual. He's got some kind of crazy girlfriend situation going on. He always does," Bryce said.

"It's that southern charm of his," Patty stated. "They attract everyone. And from South Carolina—they have such lovely manners."

She elaborated animatedly. "Southern manners are different than northern manners. They've got more flourish. It's the difference between 'Please allow me to hold the door for you, Ma'am,' and 'My *dear* lady, *may* I hold the door?' It's more like the Europeans. It's desperately chivalrous. Faced with that, *any* woman will melt." She took a sip of her tea and added, "I was a puddle when I met Horton Foote."

Susan cast a dubious glance at her, but Patty went on to describe meeting the famous playwright at a shindig down south. "He was so courtly," she said with a fond smile.

"Bryce," said Susan directly, "How was Norfolk?"

"It's good. I think I'm going to enjoy the cabin. Michael and his team are still going through the papers, of course," he said, "But it looks good."

"You need to have the roof done," Susan said.

"Why? It looks fine," Bryce protested. "Besides, do you think Grandfather would let something like that slip?"

"Grandfather wasn't well at the end. I'm telling you, have the roof done," Susan reiterated flatly.

"Okay, okay," Bryce conceded.

Patty and Bryce looked at each other. Patty, with her long straight brown hair and dangly earrings had crinkles at the corners of her eyes from smiling constantly. You could even see them behind her large-frame glasses. The walls featured her photographs; vast fields of bluebonnets and tiny red hummingbirds. As an artist, she wasn't quite what her family expected. Maybe that was why Bryce felt a kinship between them. She may have been christened Patricia Elaine Taylor Robinson, but "Patty" suited her perfectly.

There was something sad in her silence, but she knew not to countermand Susan. Bryce heard Susan and Patty having a screaming fight once back when they first started dating. They were all spending the weekend at a friend's summer house in Chatham, New York. He'd come back into the house to get an extra towel for the pool and heard them fighting in their bedroom. Patty tried to stick up for herself, but Susan verbally eviscerated her. Afterwards, he heard Patty sobbing plaintively, followed by Susan's tones, which became sincerely apologetic. She was the kind who exploded and regretted it later. The rest of the weekend, she was visibly attentive to Patty, even being demonstrably affectionate—something she never did, probably more because it wasn't like her than because she was trying to be discreet about her sexual orientation—but Bryce sensed that some sort of bitter understanding had been established. Bryce could've told Patty that things with Susan were fine as long as Susan was allowed to have her head. Having learned it most likely while he was still in diapers, it never occurred to him to warn Patty.

Susan seemed mild now as her fork cut through the thick ribbon of cream cheese frosting on the carrot cake.

"Staying for dinner? We're having steak," Susan said.

"No thanks, besides, I don't eat much red meat any more. It isn't good for you," Bryce said.

"Nonsense. That's what gives me strength," Susan explained. "Why do you think these tree-huggers can't get anything accomplished in the world? It's because they're all anemic!"

"I love Margaret's pot roast," Patty said, "But when she serves steak I usually skip it and just have extra vegetables. I really prefer chicken; like you said, it's so much healthier."

Susan was savoring a bite of cake and let the remark go. Patty seemed relieved.

They chatted for about a half hour longer, mostly Patty performing the role of the entertaining hostess, with Susan and Bryce exchanging important bits of business in the margins. When it came time to leave, Patty stayed behind after Susan announced she would walk Bryce to the door.

As always, when she stood up, she seemed taller than she was. She barely cleared his shoulder, but in his mind, he retained the impression that they were the same height. She had clear, creamy skin with a natural tinge of rosiness in the cheeks, deep blue eyes, and platinum blonde hair that she wore in a short bob. She wasn't pretty in the conventional sense. Her face was too broad, but she was stately, though she lumbered slightly when she walked, a habit their nanny and two finishing schools couldn't completely correct. As a little boy, Bryce thought she looked like Jeanne d'Arc, a figure of strength and *gravitas*; a champion.

"I'm concerned about you now that you have so many holdings," she began, walking closely beside him. "I'd like you to let me oversee things, at least until you get your bearings."

"Susan," Bryce began with a sigh, "I'm a grown man. I can handle it."

"Bryce," Susan countered, "You don't have the background. Not with all those years off on your own. I don't want you doing something stupid."

"What are you afraid of, that I'll give it all to the Hare Krishnas?" Bryce joked.

"Tell Michael to expect my call on Monday morning. I want to go over everything with him," Susan steadily instructed, lowering her voice as they approached the door where Margaret stood ready with Bryce's coat and scarf.

Susan gave Bryce a parting lean-in and lumbered back down the hallway.

Bryce turned to Margaret and thanked her for his coat. He found himself approving of her prim black dress with its crisp white collar. Susan didn't allow informal uniforms as some of his younger friends did with their staff. The ones who did were mostly *nouveau riche*, anyway, and the impression given by butlers and maids clad in ill-fitting khaki pants and button-down shirts was that of being served by the Geek Squad at Best Buy. Either that, or they were so informally dressed that they blended in with the guests.

One time, at a small party on Long Island, Bryce had given his coat to an older woman who answered the door. She was dressed in business casual. She brought him his drink and later offered a tray of canapés to him. He was shocked subsequently to see her lounging on the arm of a chair, sipping a Martini, chatting with guests.

"Isn't that a bit too familiar?" he had remarked to his date, who was a friend of the host.

"That's his mother," she whispered.

That was Long Island for you.

3

No sooner did he start the engine but a call came in from Deek.

"Bryce!" Deek greeted him joyfully.

"Deacon!" Bryce responded. "What's up?"

"Tammy got a job!"

"That's great," said Bryce. "What's she doing?"

"She's actually at work right now. She's a counter girl at CVS"

Bryce cringed inwardly but he was happy that Deek was happy, so he tried to sound elated.

"Wow, that's wonderful; I'm sure she'll be very good at it," he offered.

"That's not the best thing, though," Deek added, "Things are much better between us. I mean, she's been throwing up every day before work, but she's managed to do okay. She even says she likes the routine because it gives her life structure—the work, not the vomiting. Last night we had an amazing evening."

"I'm happy for you," Bryce said, "Especially after everything you've gone through."

"Boy, I tell you, this is a great change. Everything is going to be different now," Deek affirmed.

"I hope so, Deek, I really hope so. Look, I'm driving back from Susan's and I'm kind of beat. Can I catch up with you mid-week?"

"Sure thing. I just wanted to share the good news," Deek replied.

"Please congratulate Tammy for me and give her my regards," Bryce said.

"Will do. Safe trip," Deek said.

"Thanks," Bryce said, hanging up.

Bryce heaved a deep sigh. So Tammy the Trainwreck was now a gum-chewing twat at CVS. What was it with Deek? He was always plucking women from the bottom of the barrel. Bryce knew all too well how difficult girls from their class could be, so he could understand Deek's motivation to marry beneath him and elevate the woman. It happened all the time. Hadn't that southern billionaire even married one of his servants? It could be successfully done. But there were just as many high-strung low-class women, possibly even more so, and Deek had a talent for finding them.

Tammy had some kind of eating disorder compounded by a drinking disorder. She suffered depression, too, and would cut herself. No, wait, that was the one before; the one who had all those tattoos. What had her name been? Bryce couldn't recall. She disgusted him.

Deek agonized over Tammy's constant ups and downs. He hoped he could stabilize her life, this Caligula of a woman who couldn't tell a salad fork from a dinner fork.

Bryce surmised that Deek had spent too much time at boarding school as a kid and was emotionally stilted from not having had enough contact with his mother. They were Hilton Head folk who had lavish money. Deek's mother was mostly always away at hot springs, soaking herself during his formative years. He and Bryce met in college, by which time the damage was already done.

But Deek wasn't the only one with girlfriend troubles. Bryce was beginning to think he himself was in love with a woman who didn't return his affections.

He'd had a complicated romantic life, Bryce reasoned, and he couldn't blame it on his own mother, who was ever present and supportive. It had been his father who'd been the distant one, weak and feckless, as the sons of strong men often are. It couldn't have been easy to have been Grandfather's son, Bryce allowed, but his father was about as commanding as a bowl of oatmeal. He mumbled, he was frequently away on business, and he didn't take any particular pride in raising a son.

Bryce let his mind wander as he drove along the highway and could finally recall he and his father sailing together once. His father borrowed a friend's boat which was docked in Rye, and they set out into Long Island Sound. Twenty minutes into the adventure, Bryce's father became so seasick he had to go below. Bryce actually managed to keep the craft going for quite some time until his father finally reappeared and took the helm to bring them back in.

"Nice job, son," his father had said weakly.

In retrospect, Bryce realized it had gone a long way towards building his self-esteem, that he could manage a boat at age eleven, and it would've made him feel especially proud had he not realized the merit came through default, not intention. His father had been too lost in his own misery to really appreciate much in the world around him in general. It was a sad testament to his memory that his death had so miniscule an impact on everyone. People barely realized he was gone. Mother, of course, upheld his honor by being particularly kind and gracious when she spoke of him thereafter; it was her gently idealized version of him which Bryce preferred to remember rather than the reality.

But back to the present, there was the matter of Leslie. He should call her.

4

Stephanie was the girl he should've married.

They grew up together in Ardsley, a small town in Westchester County, New York, about half an hour north of the city. Her family was Old Money too; her grandfather had been some kind of steel magnate.

Her next-door neighbor was Topher Van Hees, a boy in their grade at school who was remarkable for his stupidity. Bryce always hated being invited over to Topher's. Not only did he suspect Topher of having designs on Stephanie, but he had completely insipid conversation skills, and a really creepy elderly maid who, as far as Bryce could tell, only ever served oxtail soup for lunch. He would try to make some excuse to get out of it, but then Stephanie would go and he'd feel obliged to go, if only to keep Topher from making any points with her.

Stephanie seemed to think kindly of Topher, even though Bryce knew she could tell he was an idiot too. Still, if he made any jokes in that regard, she would rebuke him. She was too well bred to be unkind like that. That was one of the things he admired about her.

Things with Stephanie were comfortable. They dated through high school and continued seeing each other during Bryce's first year at college. That was Stephanie's year abroad, and she sent letters faithfully from the Sorbonne, where she was doing some kind of lofty-sounding study program, but mainly she was touring Europe.

Then halfway through the year, he met Cristina.

She was the daughter of an Italian diplomat, a descendant of a family of Milanese nobility. Her great-great-somebody was Giovanni Anguissola, who built the Castle of Grazzano Visconti, and she was vaguely related to the Renaissance painter Sofonisba Anguissola.

Whereas Stephanie was bright, personable, and loyal with fresh face looks and honey-colored hair, Cristina had a touch of Continental flair about her. She didn't wear the preppy styles American girls did and wouldn't be caught dead in Topsiders. She was more feminine, preferring richly colored silk scarves, long, soft leather gloves, and the most intoxicating scent Bryce had ever experienced.

Besides, with Stephanie, he always knew where he stood. With Cristina, he always wondered. Not that she was temperamental—she was decidedly stable—but she had a way of giving a sidelong glance or saying "Oh," in such a tone of voice that it unbalanced him. He always had the feeling there was a lot more going on behind her eyes than she revealed, which is probably why it shouldn't have come as a surprise to him when she ended their relationship abruptly and became engaged to a Spanish nobleman.

"But you hate the Spanish," he protested.

"Bryce," Cristina patiently explained, "His family is very solid. I don't want an uncertain future." She kissed his cheeks sympathetically as he wept.

He had to admit that her reasoning was logical, because he had just broken away from his family and was on his own. He couldn't promise her anything but love. He felt especially bad because it hadn't been that long since he'd broken up with Stephanie to date Cristina, and now this.

Stephanie had taken it well. She'd sniffled, but maintained her composure.

"Whatever makes you happy, Bryce," she said resolutely, "I wish you all the best," and Bryce could tell that she meant it from the very depths of her soul. At the time he thought she was being a sport, but after Cristina had left him, he reflected that Stephanie must have been devastated when he ended things with her. After all, most of their peers were already paired off together. Whom would she marry? What had he done?

His enduring guilt led him to look her up about two years later. She had married Topher. They lived in Scarsdale (Topher's sister got the Ardsley house) and Topher had some kind of bank job in the city where he sat at a big walnut desk and signed blank papers all day, or just about. Bryce figured his briefcase was probably as empty as his head, but he was able to give Stephanie a proper home. He thought about calling her then, but decided against it.

Meanwhile, Cristina had kept in touch over the years. She and the Count (or whatever he was) were content. She spent a lot of time yachting in the Adriatic while he was off performing official duties.

"Are you wearing a mantilla yet?" Bryce would ask.

"Stop it, you're terrible," she would respond with annoyance. Bryce could just picture her with her petite figure and tanned skin, drinking Testa Rossas and flipping through the pages of *Donna* magazine as the yacht slowly went nowhere.

That reminded him, he owed her a call. They hadn't talked in months. Her stepdaughter was getting married to a French nobleman, and he should call to congratulate her. Cristina had done her job well.

But back after the breakup with Cristina, he had gone on a few dates with random women over the next several years, but nothing that amounted to anything. He was too busy getting his life together, which was much harder than he anticipated without family money. He and Susan had had a bit of a falling out at that time as well, so she was no help. She couldn't afford to side with Bryce because she needed to stay in Grandfather's good graces, which was becoming more difficult since he figured out that she liked girls.

It wasn't on moral grounds that he held any objection, but he thought it was vastly unwise of her to be openly gay. Back in his day, he explained, there were lesbians too, but they lived together as spinsters and presented an image to the world of two dear friends who both had the misfortune of never having received marriage proposals, and who were sharing expenses in order to make ends meet since they didn't have husbands to provide for them. Behind closed doors, they could do whatever they liked, Grandfather said, and he meant it. But Susan felt differently.

At that time, Patty was threatening to walk if Susan wouldn't marry her.

"It's easier for her because she's bohemian," Susan railed. Everyone knew artists did crazy things, so it wouldn't have shocked anyone in Patty's circle to hear she'd married a woman, but Susan didn't have that luxury. Bryce thought it was a shame that Susan was caught in such a bind, but in the end, her love for Patty won out. She didn't want to lose her. Grandfather wouldn't attend the ceremony and didn't speak to Susan for a year, but eventually he came around. He didn't want to lose Susan.

Bryce, however, was outright expendable to the old man. When Bryce announced he was sick and tired of all the strings attached to his money, Grandfather cut him loose without an argument. Now he wouldn't have to go to law school or attend galas full of entitled elitists and social bounders. He would, however, have to figure out how to make rent. Ultimately, he couldn't get any student loans and the work opportunities offered him by the department head were barely enough to cover tuition, so he had to leave school.

Word traveled fast. A lot of friends became scarce, either because they didn't want to be associated with a radical or they were afraid he'd hit them up for a loan. Deek didn't bolt, though, and Cristina could afford to stay connected to him because they were an ocean away and his actions wouldn't cast any reflection on her.

Over the next ten years, he tried his hand at a variety of work, mostly jobs that required writing skills. He discovered that in the real world, most people never learned to write properly, which shocked him. He taught History at a posh private high school for a while, which paid very well and was very gratifying until the school had to close down. So many of the families simply couldn't afford it any more. Divorce and bad management had ruined inherited fortunes that it had taken generations to create.

For a while, he actually worked as a telemarketer, selling upscale-sounding home security systems. Bryce had no confidence in the product, but it paid the bills. His colleagues were the most bizarre group of people he'd ever met. He wasn't sure if it was because they were telemarketers or if all people working low-wage jobs were like that.

Nobody could understand why he was there, given that his manners and bearing immediately betrayed his background. He made the mistake once of telling someone about his year at an Ivy League school, and then sometimes people would refer to it, which he found horrifically embarrassing.

He knew that they'd never fully accept him and that they eyed him with mistrust, but they were decent in their way. Their sophomoric jokes and fast-food culture sickened him, but he could see that they were good people. What he couldn't understand was their fierce pride in their social standing. A co-worker once expressed confusion about a point of grammar and Bryce tried to explain, only to be met with an abrasive rebuke. Why didn't the man want to learn? *Fine, go ahead and keep saying "I woulda went,"* thought Bryce.

That reminded Bryce that Patty had once mentioned that she had an acquaintance from the wrong side of the tracks who came into a bit of money and was anxious to know how to better himself. The young man literally took notes, she said, as she made suggestions, explained things, and answered questions. Patty was happy to do it but Susan always argued it was a waste of time, reasoning that the poor are that way because they want to be, and the fellow would be broke again in no time because he'd surely lapse back into old ways.

If Susan had seen the telemarketers with whom Bryce had worked, she would've been vindicated. They were an odd lot. It was no wonder they were poor. They did such stupid things with money. Lottery tickets every payday, just as regularly as Bryce was putting money in his savings account; continually buying cheap clothes that continually fell apart instead of saving for something of better quality that lasted. It was baffling. Didn't these people learn about money at home? Apparently not.

At any rate, around that time, Mother died, which effectively ended his financial problems. She was under orders from Grandfather not to give Bryce any money, but he couldn't stop her from doing it in her will. Nobody had counted on the fact that she would succumb to breast cancer at 56 years of age. Susan had done a lot for her at the end, but she had been brave, sitting by the window with her cashmere lap-robe, staring off into the distance. Bryce never asked what she was thinking.

True to form, she left detailed instructions and had handled as many arrangements as could be made ahead of time. She would be buried next to their father. Mother was practical and didn't want a fuss. She'd rather they saved their money. It was a simple funeral. Mother was an only child so Aunt Bitsy, her oldest friend, helped Susan with the catering and thank-you notes. Patty created a large montage of photographs of Mother, which Bryce thought was touching, but he could tell most mourners thought it was a bit much. True, it would've been more proper to display a single, classic, beautifully framed photo, but Bryce knew Patty was heartbroken and this was her way of paying tribute to her mother-in-law. "Her heart's in the right place," Aunt Bitsy had commented to him as they stood looking at the display, but Bryce could tell they both knew Mother wouldn't have liked it.

5

Leslie was at home when Bryce called. Leslie was always at home when she wasn't at work. She was sitting around waiting for Graham to call. Graham was married. Graham didn't call.

However, she sounded happy that someone had called, and immediately agreed to meet Bryce. When she arrived at his apartment in Larchmont, she suggested they go out for coffee.

It was five o'clock and Bryce didn't like drinking caffeine that late, but he offered to brew her some coffee himself.

"What is it with you rich guys? You're so cheap!" Leslie complained.

"It's not that I'm cheap," Bryce said, "I just don't know why we have to go out and pay four dollars a cup for coffee that I can make right here at home."

"Fine, whatever," she conceded, so Bryce ground some Zabar's beans and made coffee for them. Leslie had plucked the box of Wheat Thins from the top of his refrigerator and stuck her hand in the bag, then munched the crackers aimlessly.

"Do you have any peanut butter to go with these?" she asked with her mouth full.

Bryce smiled. Cristina thought peanut butter was revolting. He'd stopped eating it during their relationship and hadn't resumed. It never occurred to him how vulgarly American peanut butter was until Cristina had said that. It stayed with him.

"No," he answered, "But I have some pimiento cheese in the fridge."

"Never mind," she said.

Bryce knew she was feeling frustrated about Graham. He was just waiting for her to tell him the latest. He didn't have to wait long.

"Graham was supposed to call me tonight," she said with a forlorn expression. "He always does this, and we talked about it and he said he'd do better, but then he leaves me hanging."

"Leslie," Bryce said, "He's always going to leave you hanging. He's married."

"But he promised he'd carve out more time for me," she insisted.

The latest plan was that Graham was going to wait until his youngest went to college, which would not be for another four years.

Leslie met Graham two years previously. He was the supervisor of a neighboring department at the PR firm where she worked. Leslie started at the company as a temporary employee. Graham had gone out of his way to be nice to her. Little by little she got the impression he was flirting with her, so she had casually asked around the office about him, only to be told he was married, which was strange because he talked like a single man.

"Here are photos of me skiing at Vail," he'd said, offering pictures. Colleagues said he'd showed them photos of him and his wife and children skiing at Vail. "Last weekend I saw that new action movie," he'd said. Colleagues said he'd said he and his son saw that new action movie.

Leslie had fallen for him quickly. He was intelligent, handsome, and fascinating. By the time he asked her out for drinks, she was willing to do anything in order to have him. She hardly needed to be told that he and his wife hadn't been intimate for years, or that they'd grown hopelessly apart, although it was satisfying to hear it. She was the right woman for him, of that she had no doubt.

Bryce, meanwhile, had scores of doubts. He told Leslie she was being foolish, that she was naïve, and possibly a homewrecker.

"How can you trust a man who's willing to cheat on his wife?" Bryce demanded. "For all you know, she and the children are sitting home waiting for him while he's out screwing you in some cheap motel room."

"Don't be dramatic, we make love at my place," Leslie corrected.

"Love?" Bryce asked, "What love? If he loved you, he'd make an honest woman of you."

"Christ, you talk like someone out of the seventeen-hundreds! I reject the patriarchy; I have nothing to be ashamed of," Leslie said.

"Are you kidding? You're spreading your legs for the patriarchy. Graham is having his cake and eating it too. He gets to have a respectable wife and family and enjoy a piece on the side. You get nothing." Bryce looked Leslie in the eyes. "Do you honestly believe he's going to run away with you?"

Leslie started crying. Bryce was instantly sorry he'd been so blunt. He hadn't meant to hurt her. He was enraged by the thought that this bastard, Graham, was using her and she couldn't see it at all. He put his arms around her and she sobbed into his sweater. Bryce reflected that it would need to go to the dry cleaner tomorrow; Leslie wore an abundance of mascara that got everywhere when she cried. He wondered why middle-class girls wore so much makeup. It wasn't becoming.

He thought Leslie was beautiful despite the mascara that had all but ruined his sweater and was now streaming down her face. In a minute she'd look like Alice Cooper. It was always like this when they argued about Graham.

"I'm sorry," he said. "I just can't stand to see him hurt you like this."

"Graham loves me," Leslie said, choking back tears. "We're going to get through this and we're going to be together. I just have to be strong, and I have to be patient."

Bryce thought she sounded as if she were reciting some kind of mantra that had kept her hanging on this long; he realized Graham probably originated those very words.

Bryce poured a cup of coffee and handed it to Leslie. "Look," he said, "You can't have Graham, but you can have me. I'm available. Give me a chance. I think I could make you happy."

Leslie took the cup and drew a long hot sip. Bryce wondered how she could drink such hot coffee without scalding herself.

"I appreciate you, Bryce," Leslie said softly, "But I need more time. Maybe I am just fooling myself about Graham. Sometimes I wonder if he's just stringing me along, but I can't let myself think like that. If I do, what have the past two years meant?"

That's the sixty-four-thousand-dollar question, thought Bryce. *How will she feel when she finally realizes Graham is nothing but a cad? Or, as Deek would say, that he's crookeder than a dog's back leg?*

Bryce knew she was utterly deluded but he couldn't help being attracted to her. Her hair had an auburn tinge and was wavy and soft with bangs in the front. She had brown eyes and wayward eyebrows. Something about her facial expressions reminded him of an adorable terrier he had when he was a boy. His heart went out to Leslie in a way it never had with anyone else.

"Would you consider just letting me date you?" he asked.

"What do you mean?" Leslie replied.

"Just be less available to Graham for a while," Bryce explained. "Tell him you need some space. Stop screwing him. Meanwhile, go out with me. It doesn't have to be physical, let's just see if you like having me as a boyfriend."

"I can't do that," Leslie said. "Graham and I are completely open with each other. I couldn't lie to him like that."

"You mean you couldn't lie to him the way he lies to his wife?" Bryce countered.

"He does not lie to her," she said angrily.

“The hell he doesn’t,” Bryce said. “You told me he told her last month that he was away on a business convention while you two were in Lake Tahoe.”

“It wasn’t exactly a lie, he just couldn’t come out and say we were together, but he knows that she knows their marriage is over,” Leslie pleaded.

Bryce took a deep breath. Had it really come to this? Pedantic arguments with a woman who wouldn’t see sense if it hit her between the eyes? He must be in love, he reasoned.

Leslie walked over to the sofa and sat down. She took another long drink of hot coffee as Bryce watched, astonished that her mouth wasn’t burning. She could do that with soup, too. It mystified him.

“Aren’t you going to ask how my weekend was?” he asked.

“How was it?” she asked absently.

“I went up to the cabin in Norfolk. It’s all mine now,” he said.

“Nice,” Leslie said.

“I could take you there sometime,” he offered.

“Maybe,” she replied.

Bryce could tell she didn’t care. She was looking at her watch. She was probably thinking Graham might call any second and she should be back home so they could have a long romantic conversation.

“I should be going,” she said.

“Sure,” Bryce said. “Would you like me to walk you home?”

“All the way to Pelham?” she said.

“Well, I could drive you,” he said.

“I brought my car,” she told him.

“I could drive you home in it,” he suggested.

“Then how will you get home?” she asked.

“I don’t know, I’ll figure something out,” he said.

They both started laughing but it was a dry laugh, more for effect than anything else; a polite way of wrapping up an awkward conversation. Leslie kissed Bryce on the cheek and left. He watched out the window as she got in her car and drove away.

6

Suddenly, he was starving.

The tea and carrot cake he'd had at Susan's had been quickly burned off by the emotional turmoil he'd just experienced with Leslie. Conflict always made him hungry.

On Sunday night, he liked to have sandwiches or other light meals, usually because he'd had a huge Sunday midday dinner. However, tonight he wanted something substantial. The weather had just begun to get crisp and he felt like having chicken pot pie.

When he was little, their maid, Delia, had baked the most delicious chicken pot pies he'd ever tasted. The crust was buttery and flaky, enclosing moist chunks of chicken and fresh potatoes, carrots, and peas, swimming in a rich, flavorful gravy.

He didn't feel like dining out and he didn't feel like cooking. He decided on Indian from the place around the corner. Indian food, for some reason, reminded him of Delia's Irish cuisine. Everything was stew. He opted for Lamb Rogan Josh, served with a container of wholesome steamed basmati rice.

As he ate the warm, comforting dinner, he recalled that his friend Rohan laughed the first time he told him about how Indian food reminded him of Irish food. Rohan was a Brahmin whose family owned an immense cashew plantation back home. Indians gave new meaning to the term Old Money. Bryce's family fortune went back a few hundred years; Rohan's went back thousands. Bryce used to kid Rohan that he was still probably drawing off a trust fund set up for him by Genghis Khan.

"You're mad, do you know that?" Rohan would laugh, "Totally mad."

7

Bryce slept well and woke up feeling refreshed. It was Monday. He liked Mondays.

He went for a quick jog. He passed the apartment building where Lou Gehrig lived. It was modest by modern standards—extremely so for a sports star—but they didn't pay them that much in those days. Gehrig bought a house later, but he didn't have long to live in it.

The older Bryce got, the more he appreciated history, especially local history. Things that seemed hokey when he was younger became significant. Who lived in that apartment now? Did they know that Gehrig was the former tenant? Did they know who Gehrig even was? And if they did, would they care?

Bryce had gone into a small tobacconist's shop once and was overcome with the scent of several rich and gorgeous blends. "That's beautiful," he remarked to the owner.

"Back in Pakistan," the owner replied, "We have a saying: 'A lovely thing has no value unless there is someone there to appreciate it.' Today you are here to appreciate it." Bryce smiled; the thought pleased him.

When he returned from his jog, he showered and checked messages. Leslie left a message that Graham had apologized to her at the office that morning and vowed to make it up to her for having not contacted her during the weekend. It was all okay, Leslie explained, his in-laws had dropped in unannounced and his father-in-law had to be taken to the emergency room for chest pains. It turned out to be nothing, but it ruined his plans to connect with her.

In short, Leslie felt that she and Graham were back on track and she wanted to disavow her temporary apparent disloyalty to him. She reiterated to Bryce that he was a good friend, and nothing more. She begged him to dismiss her momentary loss of faith in the man she loved.

"It happens," Bryce wrote back, shaking his head.

Bryce had never met Graham but he got the clear impression he was a pompous ass. He was a small man who wanted to think he was a big man. He probably really believed that he was as brilliant and cultured as he portrayed himself to be, and women like Leslie were too ignorant to know the difference.

"He drives a Volvo," she'd remarked once with obvious admiration, as though that were the definitive mark of a man of distinction. Coming from a world filled with mediocre mid-range cars, it would seem that way to her, Bryce figured. Or how she once reported, almost breathlessly, that Graham had taken her to a romantic little Greek place in Tarrytown and ordered saganaki for her. The platter of flaming cheese that was served to them was about the most impressive thing she'd ever seen in a restaurant, and she was awed by Graham's worldliness. Then again, she was the kind of person who was impressed by gimmicky franchises like Rainforest Cafe, the very thought of which made Bryce almost physically ill with disdain.

Like those awful people who celebrate their birthday at The Cheesecake Factory. He shuddered involuntarily at the thought.

Graham was simply a half-step above that, but he was an easy sell to a woman who was dissatisfied with the mundanity of being middle-class, and who strove to broaden her horizons.

Bryce, on the other hand, tried to fulfill this goal by first encouraging her to read. She read mostly tripe—soppy romances and trite detective stories—the kind Bryce wished he had on hand every time he kindled a fire. She dismissed good classics as "boring." Bryce had concurred that brilliant things were often boring, citing Einstein's theories as a prime example. However, he maintained that intellectual concepts, once digested, contributed to both a new perspective on life and a ready ability to generate sophisticated conceptions of one's own. It was up to the individual reader to hunt and mine these concepts within great literature.

He cited *Crime and Punishment* as an illustration during their discussion.

"Dostoyevsky's writing is dry and dull. You wade through pages and pages of it. It seems like it will never end. Then suddenly, *behold!* You discover a nugget of wisdom that you will always treasure," he explained.

Leslie remained unconvinced. Bryce had to accept that she didn't have the mental discipline he was fortunate to have had instilled in him by a private-school education, and at 28, she was too old to change.

All these thoughts occurred to him in the instant before he sent his reply to Leslie's e-mail. Maybe he was trying to construct some interior objection to his affection for her. It was an attempt to do something with his mind that he couldn't quite do with his heart. He sighed got on with his day.

He had a few things to mail, so he walked down to the post office. Bryce loved going there because they had a WPA mural on the wall. Many New York towns did, a testament to the Works Progress Administration which was initiated by President Franklin Delano Roosevelt in response to the Great Depression. Artists were hired by the government to paint murals inside post offices, generally depicting historic scenes from American history. The caliber of talent varied from town to town, but overall, they were passably good, if not excellent. But that wasn't the point—it was the heartwarming idea that millions of Americans of all walks of life, including artists, were being celebrated and supported as vital to the nation. Bryce felt the same kind of patriotic well-being when he saw these murals as he did when he lit sparklers on the Fourth of July. He wasn't a flag-waver, he said to himself, but certain things stirred his national pride.

Bryce left the post office and walked down Boston Post Road to his apartment. He reflected that this was the same postal route along which mail had been transported along for centuries. He was pleased that he lived in New York. So many of his contemporaries, also descended from old money families, had chosen to adapt to changing social and economic conditions by relocating their primary residence to various locations—Litchfield County, Connecticut; Sussex County, New Jersey; even northern Virginia. True, it was there they would find many others of their ilk, but Bryce felt New York was the place to be. Becoming part of the Old Money diaspora was not for him. For one thing, he didn't own a proper house; Grandfather's cottage in Norfolk was the first piece of real estate he'd ever acquired.

Unfortunately, the prices of the traditional residence areas had become so inflated that unless his peers inherited a house (and even if they had, the taxes alone were prohibitive), they weren't able to afford it, except for a few old holdouts who positively refused to budge. One of his former classmates from Ardsley was like that. She grew up in Westchester, and she was staying in Westchester, even if it killed her. Her husband worked for a major investment firm in the city. They had no children, so that saved a lot of money. Even so, they had to be terribly thrifty. Bryce saw a recent photo of her in an event dress that he remembered from when they were teens.

Meanwhile, others left and settled for the next best thing in terms of location. His friend John grew up in Saddle River (about the only worthwhile area of New Jersey, at least from a New Yorker's point of view), but he couldn't afford to live there, so he made his home in Lake Mohawk in the wilderness northwest of NYC. Bryce had never heard of the area at that point because there was nothing to hear about; it was the boonies. But it was clean, safe, and affordable—if something of a hike to civilization—and still close enough for John to visit his Old Holdout friends in Saddle River.

The carpetbaggers, however, were a real puzzle. Migrating to formerly hokey redneck states like Virginia, West Virginia, Georgia, and South Carolina, the big draw for them was that for the same money that would buy a tiny condo in their native area, they could buy a six-bedroom McMansion on four acres with a three-car garage and a barn for the horses. If they had enough Old Money neighbors, it was almost like being back home, but cheaper and with less snow. (And with all the money they could save, they were able to take posh skiing trips to Vermont every winter.) Still, Bryce wondered how they ever adapted to a lesser existence.

And of course, some acquaintances had chosen to move to the land of the early-bird special a few decades early, which seriously puzzled Bryce. They headed for the elephant burial ground of all New Yorkers: Florida. Obviously, they couldn't afford Palm Beach (too much new money) so they joined their fellow Old Money folks in West Palm Beach. The lifestyle was decidedly relaxed for those in their mid-thirties, but they coped by taking up knitting and shuffleboard and that sort of thing. Mostly though, they would while away the afternoons sitting beside their pools, drinking mojitos and making granny-square blankets they'd never be able to use. It was decidedly boring, but it beat struggling to make ends meet, and they got a year-round tan.

Bryce primarily considered himself basically an Old Holdout (without the house) but enjoyed having the cottage in Connecticut. The area there was too cultured to be boonie, but too sparsely populated to be chic, and definitely too low-profile to be prestigious. The one word on everyone's lips was *quaint*. Every antique shop in the county had at least two spinning wheels for sale. An astonishing number of his old high school friends from Ardsley and environs moved to the area after being priced out of the market in their hometowns by new money.

But of course, there was one old classmate who fell into another category entirely: she was a traitor. She married a hedge-fund manager and lived on the Upper East Side.

By now, he was back at his flat and the phone was ringing. Locking the door and tossing his jacket aside, he answered. It was Cricket. He was sorry he'd been exuberant enough not to let the answering machine get it. He couldn't stand Cricket.

"Bryce," she said, "It's Cricket. I need to talk to you."

"Hi," he replied. "What's up?" He didn't know what the answer would be, but he was already dreading it.

Cricket began to recount some need of some club with which she was affiliated and with which he was formerly affiliated before he could no longer afford the membership fees. She was on some kind of board or committee (she was always in charge of something, which suited her bossy personality perfectly) and she called to badger him for money or guilt him into doing some messy favor to sustain this entity.

Bryce wasn't really paying attention, instead preferring to survey the greenery in his apartment. The ivy atop his bookshelf was doing well, but he had a fern that had been lingering unhealthily for months.

Plants die a slow death, he thought. He returned to the conversation in progress as Cricket stridently denounced members who weren't contributing enough to upkeep and were behind in their dues.

"I'm talking about you, Bryce," she said in summation.

"Oh, right. Yes; well," he struggled to come up with a way of saying he had no intention of giving any of his time or money to whatever it was she was calling about in such a manner that it sounded imperially dismissive rather than motivated by distaste for her and her club. He wanted her to hang up thinking, "Well, that's me told," instead of "Cheap bastard."

He quickly settled on ". . . at this time there haven't been any allocations for this kind of support," swiftly adding "I am sympathetic, though," in as sincere a tone as he could muster.

"That's simply not good enough," Cricket shot back in obvious annoyance.

"I'm afraid it'll have to be," Bryce countered.

Unfazed, Cricket went for the jugular. "You've recently come into an inheritance," she stated. "Don't you think your grandfather would want standards to be maintained? Don't you think he'd be ashamed of your completely thoughtless behavior in turning your back on your responsibilities like this?"

Bryce was stung both by her audacity and by the truth of what she'd just said. Yes, Grandfather would be outraged to see him being so flippant, imperiling his reputation so heedlessly. But Grandfather was sitting on millions by the time he was 20; at the point he'd reached Bryce's age, he was managing an empire. Cricket's grandfather founded a chain of department stores which still provided her with an incredibly lucrative income, not to mention the fortune into which she'd prudently married. She could well afford to shame Bryce for his failings. With a sigh, Bryce realized that being excoriated for his shortcomings as a member of polite society was the price he had long ago determined to pay for his freedom. Nevertheless, it was an ugly business.

For a fleeting moment, guilt motivated Bryce to consider using a portion of his new inheritance just to get Cricket off his back, but he steeled his resolve. At this point, it wasn't just about the money; it was about the principle. He saw no reason to subsidize outdated bastions of cultural superiority. These leagues of empty-headed standard-bearers were so busy drawing up restrictive roles for admissions that they failed to realize nobody wanted in any more. They didn't even discern how desperate they looked, like Cricket, who'd come begging for money. With a flush of pride, he realized it was she who should be ashamed.

Unfortunately, there was no polite way of saying "You're pathetic and irrelevant." However, he could always fall back on the longstanding tradition of putting number one first. Nobody could argue with that.

"Cricket, dear," he soothed, impressed by how suavely he said it, "I've had to make many difficult decisions recently. Again, so sorry to disappoint you."

"You've been on very shaky ground for a long time," Cricket observed bitterly. "I've been standing up for you when people said you ought to be dropped—or worse." (Bryce wondered what she meant by *that*; burning a giant dollar-sign on his front lawn? A mob hit, perhaps?) "It's absolutely clear to me now that you didn't deserve any of my help and you never did. You're a total disgrace. The committee will not forget this, Bryce—not ever," Cricket darkly threatened in closing.

"I'm sure they won't," Bryce agreed, adding "Do try to have a good day."

Cricket hung up. Bryce felt relieved and sadly nostalgic. There was something about his club memberships that he loved. The rolling golf courses, the civilized brunches, the elegant events at which he knew he would be sheltered from the great unwashed. How could he love something and hate it at the same time?

Before he could pursue this line of reasoning, there was a pounding at the door. Bryce looked out the peephole to see Leslie, looking upset.

He opened the door and Leslie fell into his arms sobbing.

"My God, what is it?" he said, startled. He drew her into the room and closed the door behind her. No use treating the neighbors to her personal drama.

"There's another woman!" Leslie cried, choking out great floods of tears.

"Another woman? Bryce asked. "You mean besides Graham's wife and you?"

Leslie reached out and slapped his arm angrily. He hadn't meant to be sarcastic, but it was almost impossible not to be.

"Yes!" Leslie screamed. "At work!"

"Speaking of work, why aren't you there?" Bryce asked. "You e-mailed me from your office this morning, didn't you?"

"Yes," Leslie explained. "That's where I found out. Graham and I made up and I wrote you." She paused to cough several times and wipe her nose on her sleeve. Bryce winced. "Then I went to tell him about my plans for us for this weekend and there she was!" she said hatefully, commencing her crying-jag again.

"There *who* was?" Bryce asked.

"The other woman!" Leslie yelled, as if Bryce were stupid (and as if his walls were made of solid concrete, which they certainly weren't). He worried lest the neighbors hear the commotion.

"Easy—calm down now. No need to yell. I know who you meant, I was just asking who she is, this other woman. She's a colleague?" he asked.

"Yes. Romy Podrasky from marketing!" Leslie explained. "I saw them together! Who knows how long this has been going on?"

Bryce needed clarification. “You saw them having sex? In his office?”

“No, stupid! But she was leaning over his desk and he was looking at her and then they had their hands on each other’s arms, and I could just tell—I could just tell!” Leslie stated.

“Could it have been something innocent, like they were congratulating each other on a good project or something?” Bryce asked.

“No, not at all. Not with her touching him like that. It was very intimate, both of them!” She began to calm down a little, anger beginning to seethe in and mingle with heartbreak.

“Leslie, let me get you a class of water,” Bryce offered as Leslie sat down.

“No. I don’t need anything. I just can’t—I mean I absolutely cannot believe—that Graham would do this,” Leslie said, looking tired and bewildered.

“If you don’t mind my saying so, this can’t be that big of a shock. He’s cheating on his wife with you. Where’s the mental leap required to see that you’re not the only one?” Bryce asked.

“But it’s not like that,” Leslie insisted. “Graham is leaving his wife, he’s in a relationship with me. Romy is the woman he’s cheating with—cheating on *me* with.”

Bryce wanted to point out that technically, he was cheating on his wife with both Leslie and Romy (and who knows who else) and that all the girlfriends were on equal footing, but he knew that would send Leslie over the edge. It was as if the only comforting things he could sincerely say would be the most hurtful since she was so out of touch with reality.

He took a deep breath. She had begun crying again, but softly this time.

“So you took the day off?” he asked.

“Basically, yeah,” she said.

It made Bryce angry that this clown upset her to the point that she couldn’t even do her job. He wanted to punch him in the head. Graham wasn’t even worth a sick-day, and Leslie got few enough of them as it was.

“Oh God, Bryce, what am I doing to do?” Leslie wailed.

“Does Graham know you saw him and Romy together?” he asked.

“Yes,” she said.

“You made it sound like they were so fixated on one another; maybe he didn’t even notice you in his doorway,” he suggested.

“No, he knows. I walked in and called him a lying bastard and told Romy she was a filthy whore,” she said.

"Wow," Bryce said, realizing the whole office would be abuzz with the scandal now. How was it that people like Leslie couldn't contain their personal lives with a bit of well-placed discretion? Nevertheless, he continued. "Has Graham tried to contact you?"

"No," answered Leslie, checking her phone and shaking her head.

Bryce knew that was a bad sign, since it meant Graham wasn't innocent (or he would've called to explain) and wasn't sorry (or he would've called to apologize). Either way, it meant he had little regard for Leslie, but then again, that was obvious from the get-go with this mess. Bryce figured Graham would wait for Leslie to contact him, and then somehow place the blame for the affair on her doorstep, saying if she'd been a better girlfriend, his head wouldn't have been turned by Romy. It also occurred to Bryce that this was good news for his own prospects, because Graham probably preferred Romy to Leslie and was simply keeping the latter around as backup, but his affections had likely shifted to the whore from marketing.

"So, Romy's pretty slutty, huh?" he said, hoping to make Leslie smile.

"Yes," she whined. "She wears short dresses and heels to work every day, even Fridays."

"Well, if that's the kind of woman Graham prefers, then he certainly doesn't deserve you," he said, thinking he was paying her a compliment. Instead, he discovered he'd sparked Leslie's concerns.

"Prefers? What do you mean 'prefers'? You think he's dumping me for her?" Her eyes widened with fear and Bryce realized he'd accidentally revealed too much of Graham's playbook, the contents of which were obvious to everyone but Leslie.

Bryce stumbled a bit, then came out with the truth, unable to do otherwise. "Honestly? I think he's an unfaithful character to begin with and he's going to go through many women before he's done."

"Wait a minute, wait a minute," Leslie positioned herself on the sofa so that she could look Bryce full in the face. "So you think that he's cheating on me with other women besides Romy?"

"Leslie, I think that you're not the first woman he's cheated on his wife with, and you won't be the last. I don't think he's going to leave his wife for Romy any more than he was ever going to leave his wife for you." Bryce paused so she could take it all in, which appeared to be a challenge for her. "Don't you see? He's not having a relationship with you. Men who have relationships aren't simultaneously involved with one—or more—other persons. Graham is."

"But he takes me on trips. We make love. He *tells* me he loves me," she stated emphatically, as though it were convincing evidence.

Do I really have to explain this? Bryce thought to himself. And if so, where to begin? Should he start off with "There's this thing called cheating on your spouse," or "Unfortunately, while some people are good, there are others who are bad"? Diagrams might be required. He glanced around for a pen.

"Bryce, Graham is the love of my life. I can't not love him," she said mournfully.

"And the misfortune of love is that the person you love doesn't always love you back," Bryce said simply. Something inside him ached when he said it.

There was a moment of weighted silence.

"I want to get fucked up," said Leslie dejectedly.

"Harming yourself isn't going to solve anything and it's not going to get back at Graham," Bryce advised.

"Yeah? Well, maybe when I call him from a bar and he hears how wasted I am, he'll understand how I feel," she concluded.

"Graham doesn't give a tinker's damn how you feel; that's the point you keep missing," Bryce said.

"We'll see," she said, getting up and making a beeline for the door.

"Whoa, whoa—where are you going?" Bryce asked.

"I don't know. Someplace where I can drink myself into a coma," she said, reaching for the doorknob.

"Not that there's any shortage of such places, but getting intoxicated before—" (Bryce looked down at his watch) "—eleven AM just isn't done unless you want people to think you're on the skids. And you're not. I'm not going to let you do this to yourself. I care about you too much."

Leslie abruptly turned to Bryce and kissed him. Out of instinct, he threw his arms around her and kissed back, at first gently and then more ardently. A moment later, she broke away from him and had the door open before he knew what was happening.

"I'll show him," she said, her tear-rimmed eyes filled with hate. Before Bryce could figure out if the hate was for Graham or herself, she was gone.

8

Not even noon, and the day is already in shambles, Bryce thought.

Leslie's kiss had at first given him false—very false—hope that she had suddenly realized his superiority in comparison with the two-timing (or was it now three-timing?) Graham, but clearly it was an act of revenge, as if Graham would ever know that she'd been momentarily unfaithful.

Bryce was surprised that he himself cared about the situation at all. Sadly, he noted that he didn't care enough to chase Leslie down and save her from herself. He probably should; as a gentleman, it would be the right thing to do, and he did consider himself a gentleman. Then again, the kind of women he was supposed to gravitate towards would never do anything like this. His eyes rested on the phone and his thoughts turned to earlier that morning. Would Cricket ever do anything like this? Not on her life. She'd never waste time screwing around with a married man who was feeding her a pack of lies. Cristina? Not unless a considerable fortune were involved (like, a Middle Eastern oil fortune), and even then, probably not, if only because she had too much self-respect. And certainly not Stephanie. The very thought was ludicrous. She'd married Topher Van Hees, for God's sake, and was at home in Scarsdale, probably arranging flowers at this very moment. She'd no sooner get tangled up with a married man than . . . Bryce couldn't even fathom anything bizarre enough to complete the thought.

Talking to someone about this would be wise. Susan was clearly out because she would never understand. Patty was sympathetic and would probably be helpful, but she'd tell Susan and then Bryce would be in trouble. Susan would be furious.

About the only person left was Deek. Going to Deek for relationship advice—that was a new low. Bryce couldn't justify it. Besides, he was the one who gave Deek advice; advice Deek never took.

What about Rohan? thought Bryce. It had been a while since they'd talked. Rohan was in Chicago doing some kind of real estate business. But maybe there would be a cultural disconnect. *They have arranged marriages*, he reasoned; *they don't have to go through this stuff.*

Nevertheless, it would be good to see how Rohan was doing. Bryce placed the call.

"Hello, Bryce; how are you doing?" Rohan asked when he finally answered.

"Very well," Bryce lied. "How are things going in Chicago?"

"I'm back in New York. I had some real estate deals to handle. It's all good."

"We should get together soon, then," Bryce said. "I need your advice about something." Bryce was sorry he'd said it as soon as the words left his mouth.

"Advice? I think you need advice about a lot of things, but I'm glad you're open to taking any," Rohan said, the beginnings of his manic laughter stirring. That sound never failed to cheer Bryce.

Feeling better, Bryce continued. "I'm friends with this woman who's dating a married man and she just found out this morning that he's cheating on her with someone else; she's really devastated and probably out drinking herself blind at the moment. The catch is that I have feelings for her."

Rohan's laughter erupted. It was a volatile combination of mirth, sarcasm, and insanity, like a little boy's giggles that had been zapped with nuclear radiation so that it became a Godzilla of hilarity.

"You have feelings for this woman?" he asked, incredulous, as he continued to laugh.

"Yes. I know, it's crazy," Bryce admitted dismissively.

"Bryce—you are mad! Do you know that? You are totally mad!" There was more laughter. "How are you having feelings for this woman? She's clearly unstable. What in the world could you possibly find attractive about that?"

Bryce didn't feel like creating a laundry-list of Leslie's few good qualities, only to send Rohan into refreshed gales of giddiness. What he really wanted was advice about whether or not to find Leslie and stop her from getting drunk.

"I don't know why I like her," Bryce finally responded, "But I'm concerned about her welfare. Should I go and find her and get her to stop drinking?"

"Man, look," said Rohan, finally simmering down to a low chortle, "You're bloody crazy if you think you're going to stop her from behaving stupidly. She's an adulteress; she knows what comes with the territory. She should've anticipated this. And as for you," he added, "you're bloody crazy if you want to win her affection. My advice is to stay away. Seriously; stay away."

"Do you ever wish your family would let you date?" Bryce asked.

"Not when I hear stories like this, no," Rohan said, and Bryce couldn't quite tell if he were about to start laughing again.

"When will I see you?" Bryce asked.

"I'm meeting up with some friends in Boston the rest of this week, but possibly when I get back. And I'm telling you, you jolly well better stay away from that woman in the meantime. What else are you up to?" Rohan asked.

"Still getting things settled with Grandfather's estate. Susan's involved now; she wants to make sure I don't do anything stupid," Bryce explained.

This intelligence caused Rohan to explode in laughter anew. "I wonder why?" he gasped, hardly able to speak.

Bryce knew that Rohan's life was stiff and structured, so being able to be silly and fun like this wasn't an insult; rather, it was a testament to their closeness that Rohan felt comfortable being his real self around Bryce. Still, given the gravity of the situation with Leslie, Bryce was becoming mildly irritated with Rohan's jocularity.

"Anyway, I should get going. Thanks for the advice," Bryce said.

Rohan caught his breath and blurted "Hey, you listen to me—don't do anything stupid!" before bursting into a fit of crazed giggling. Rohan was at this point utterly lost in his own merriment, and Bryce knew from long experience that there was no talking him down.

"I won't, I promise. Take care; call me when you get back in town," Bryce said. He heard the sound of unmitigated laughter and finally a brief "Bye!" from Rohan. It was probably all he could manage to say. Bryce hung up.

If he weren't so worried about Leslie, Rohan's levity would've put him in a better mood.

Back to the problem at hand, he knew if he tried calling Leslie, she wouldn't answer. There was a bar on his block, but she probably wouldn't go there since it was more posh than hipster and she only liked to drink in cheap hipster-type places. For Leslie, a wine bar was something she considered classy (which Bryce found disturbing) so she wouldn't go to one of those to drown her sorrows. If it were him, he'd hit a good old Irish dive-bar where nobody tried to talk to you and the bartender wouldn't even serve a watered whiskey, but Leslie would be drinking something nauseating and fruit-flavored; the kind of abomination Bryce imagined they served at cocktail parties in hell when they ran out of wine coolers. Her most likely venue of choice was a trendy bar in Pelham that had a filthy men's room where one of the stalls was perpetually filled with crates of Knox gelatin, sloppily covered with a shower curtain.

Bryce made himself a quick Nutella sandwich to sustain him on his mission of mercy and set out for Pelham.

9

Pelham depressed Bryce. It was basically the Bronx, but without the magic of being an actual borough. Staten Island was like that too, but even being an actual borough wasn't enough to save it. Then again, Staten Island was beyond help. They put the bodies of the victims of the September 11th attacks there. That said it all.

Bryce had no idea what he'd say to Leslie or how he'd convince her to leave the bar once he found himself standing outside it, but he had to try. First, though, he had to find her.

He walked in and his eyes slowly adjusted to the dim lighting. He knew everyone was probably staring at him the way people do when you walk into a bar during broad daylight, as if you stumbled into an opium den. Only the most hopeless addicts were there at this hour. He didn't see Leslie.

Eventually, he could distinguish a well-toned bartender who was mostly bald with tattoos all over both arms and multiple earrings and other facial piercings. He'd definitely come to the right place; this was Leslie's drinking-hole.

"What can I get you?" asked the bartender. Bryce wondered if he looked like he needed a drink badly enough to order anything in this godforsaken place.

"Actually, I'm here looking for a friend. She's in her late twenties, shoulder-length wavy auburn hair with bangs and brown eyes," Bryce said.

"Yeah, she was here," the bartender said. "You just missed her, about five minutes ago."

Bryce mentally calculated that she wouldn't have been there that long, and became concerned that she'd perhaps pounded a large quantity of drinks in order to get drunk enough in so short a time.

"I hate to ask this," he said to the bartender, "But had she had a lot to drink? She had some upsetting news today."

The bartender smirked oddly before answering. "Just two Appletinis, but she didn't leave alone."

Bryce was stunned. So Leslie left—not plastered—in the company of another man. "Is he a regular?" Bryce asked, trying to get some kind of bearing on whom she'd picked up.

"Yeah; tough guy. But he's little. Drinks here a lot." He added "Hey—I'm sorry," probably assuming that Bryce was Leslie's boyfriend and they'd had a fight. *Inside every low-end bartender is a frustrated therapist*, Bryce reminded himself.

"Don't worry about it; thanks," Bryce said as he returned to the glaring light of day, with no idea where Leslie had gone with this diminutive thug she'd chosen to be her partner in exacting moot revenge on a married man who'd thrown her over for the office bicycle. Rohan was right; he was totally mad.

He decided not to go to Leslie's apartment. She was a grown woman and if she wanted to sleep with a stranger she picked up in a bar, she had every right to do so. She knew she could always turn to Bryce for help, and she'd already walked out of his place after breaking the news of Graham's new affair, so clearly, she didn't want further intervention. If he'd have been able to catch her in the act of inebriating herself, that would've been a good deed on his part, but at this point, he decided to stay away from the whole thing. She knew where he was if she wanted to talk.

Driving back to Larchmont he was angry without knowing why. He felt better when he got into town. Probably just being in Pelham had ruined his mood. It tended to do that. The whole place must've been built on a giant ancient Native American burial ground and was probably glowing with bad karma. He shivered inadvertently at the thought.

Bounding up the stairs to his apartment, he decided to get on with his day and if Leslie called, she called. If not, well; he hoped she'd call.

About an hour later as he was absorbed reading the latest copy of *The American Scholar*, the phone rang. He picked it up quickly. It was Aunt Bitsy.

"Bryce," she said sweetly, "I'm so glad I reached you at home. I wonder if you'd have luncheon with me next week. I promised your mother I'd look in on you from time to time and it's been a while, hasn't it?"

"Yes," Bryce admitted, finding it strange that people of his parents' generation still used the word "luncheon." A lot of their vocabulary struck him as dated. But nobody was as bad as his great-uncle's wife, who still actually used the term "colored" for African-Americans. At least it was better than the uglier alternatives.

"Did you know that they're doing *The Fantasticks* next month at that theatre I like—you know, the one with the seating that isn't too steep?" Aunt Bitsy asked. She had vertigo and was too thrifty to pay for expensive seats so she usually bought theatre tickets in the highest balcony. However, since New York City theatres were much taller than they were wide, the seats were invariably steeper than an Aztec pyramid, and over the years, Aunt Bitsy had narrowly avoided disaster on more occasions than Bryce cared to recall. She became dizzy and nearly pitched headlong to the ground floor at a classical guitar concert when she stumbled on the way to her seat and practically rolled right over the edge of the balcony, which was fitted with only a flimsy foot-high railing. It had created quite an embarrassing scene.

Why was Aunt Bitsy surprised that a theatre was doing *The Fantasticks* around Christmastime? It seemed like practically every theatre was doing *The Fantasticks* around Christmastime. The reason, however, was unfathomable to Bryce. *The Fantasticks* was a horrible show, except for "Try to Remember," the only song that made it tolerable, not unlike how everyone sat through *Turandot* to hear "Nessun dorma." It was something unbearably beautiful set in the midst of a wasteland.

Bryce agreed to get tickets for Aunt Bitsy for a December matinee; meanwhile, she'd make a reservation for their luncheon at the Woman's Club. He knew she liked showing him off to her friends, and that she also hoped to do a bit of furtive matchmaking. Past attempts had failed, but he was game nonetheless, mostly because he had such fondness for her.

"Well, I hope this isn't too short notice for next week, but I miss you," she said. Generally, people's social calendars were planned a year in advance (two, if they were really important) and nobody gave less than two weeks' notice for anything, so she clearly felt she needed to give an excuse for letting her standards slip, even though Bryce didn't think of it that way.

"No need for an apology, Aunt Bitsy; I miss you too. I'll look forward to next week," Bryce told her.

After he hung up, he didn't feel like getting back into the article he was reading, well-written though it was. *The American Scholar* was like a printed version of NPR; they would take some story that nobody could ever possibly be interested in and present it in such a way that you were on the edge of your seat, thirsting to hear more about the migratory patterns of moths in the United Kingdom. Still, he was becoming restless and worried about Leslie. What if the thug killed her? At least the bartender could provide a good description.

After having a cup of afternoon tea and fielding an inconsequential call from his lawyer, Bryce felt increasingly restless, which wasn't like him, he realized. This was because of Leslie; all because he'd gotten mixed up in her love triangle, which had now become a square. That's the way it always went. He should've seen it coming.

Given that he had no way to augment it into a pentagon, he would just stay on the sidelines and wait for her to call.

After a tense evening, the call did come after 11PM. Leslie sounded peaceful but tired. She was at home having napped for a few hours. Bryce wondered how honest she'd be about what happened since he knew the truth, but she told him everything. She'd gone back to the guy's place and they'd gotten hammered and screwed like crazed weasels.

Bryce shouldn't have been shocked, but the news was like a slap in the face nonetheless. He gathered himself and asked "So, are you going to waltz into Graham's office tomorrow and tell him or did you make a video you can send?"

"I'm not going to tell him at all," Leslie replied.

"What?" Bryce exclaimed. "Then what was the point?"

"It's for me; I'll know I slept with someone else," she said.

"That doesn't even make sense, and even if it did, in that case, why didn't you just sleep with me? I do have a penis, you know," he sneered.

"You're my friend, I couldn't sleep with you," she answered. "Anyway, it's over and now I can face whatever I have to."

Bryce was dumbfounded. "You mean like the STD test I hope you're getting tomorrow?"

"No, like forgiving Graham," she said.

"Are you crazy?" he asked. "Leslie, you don't even know if he wants to be with you anymore and regardless, he doesn't deserve you."

"No, he wants to be with me," she said happily. "He texted me tonight. He said he was just looking for some excitement and Romy basically threw herself at him. He's only human."

Bryce was grateful Leslie wasn't there in the room with him or he would've slapped her for being so stupid. He took a deep breath. "So cheating on his wife with one colleague isn't exciting enough for him? It requires two to really spark things up? And just because a woman offers herself to a man doesn't mean he has to accept—just so you know. It's not that Graham is 'only human.' In fact, the more you tell me about him, I'm beginning to believe he's not human at all because he doesn't give a damn about you or your feelings."

"Bryce," Leslie said in that superlative tone she used when she mistakenly thought she was being smart and mature, "There are some things that two people just know about each other, and I know that Graham loves me. Maybe you're not the kind who could forgive, but I am."

"I wish you and Graham every happiness then," Bryce snarled. "And luck. You'll need it. Good night." He hung up.

He attempted to read an article about the history of coffee prices in the Middle East, but his mind kept wandering. He finally turned out the lights and went to bed.

10

The rest of the week passed fitfully but uneventfully. Bryce didn't hear from Leslie at all, which was unusual. He hoped the silence was evidence of her happiness, but he suspected it was just a symptom of a greater misery that was yet to be revealed.

Still, he kept busy attending to some matters having to do with the cottage on Norfolk; Susan had made him a to-do list and knew if he didn't complete it, she would be harsh with him. He was grateful for the distraction and the feeling of accomplishment as he checked the items off one by one.

As he drove back from Connecticut on Sunday afternoon, he reflected on his situation. His new fortune was still composed of many unknowns. At the very least, his lawyer assured him he'd be looking at several million; not a grand fortune by any measure, but certainly more than he'd ever had, and he was grateful for it. There were also some rental properties in the Midwest that it might make sense to sell, and their worth was in the process of being determined.

He was excited at the prospect of investing and had announced he would be making the decisions himself, much to the consternation of the family financial advisor. Bryce noticed that the types who managed large accounts were generally ultra-conservative and had no imagination. One only had to look at their neckties to see that. Obviously, there was a place for the tried-and-true in every investment portfolio, but he believed investing was just that—a way of funding new companies and ideas.

What little engagement he'd had in investments over the years had paid off very well. He followed a small list of principles that had never failed to work. One of the greatest was "It doesn't ring a bell when it hits the top." Too many of his friends had lost their shirts when they hung on to a rising stock, anticipating it to rise yet higher. Another was "Don't be greedy." After clearing a decent profit-margin, Bryce would take his earnings and leave. At times, this had cost him even higher profits, but it had also saved him from devastating losses, and he felt that was a more-than-fair trade. A principle that invariably delighted him was "Always play with the house's money." After making a profit, Bryce would withdraw his initial investment and continue to speculate with the money his money had made; in this way, all of his investments were self-funding and only required temporary use of his own money. Finally, there was the admonition that was hardest for him to follow: "Don't let fear of missing out make you buy high." A couple of times he'd purchased a stock, only to discover 72 hours later that he could've bought 300 more shares for the same money if he'd only been patient. But overall, his financial decisions were sound and he'd done very well with very little, a bit of natural intuition, and a high tolerance level for risk. He reasoned that low-risk investments were basically bank accounts and that the whole idea of investment was that one sought greater returns. Fortunately for Bryce, he got them.

He thought of stopping over to Susan's and reviewing his progress on her to-do list for the cottage but Patty had sent him an e-mail warning him that someone from Cricket's committee who knew Susan had contacted her and mentioned his lapse in support. (Cricket probably urged them to do it—she was that kind of bitch.) Patty didn't know much more than that, but it was enough to make Bryce want to keep his distance. No use putting himself in her path if she decided to storm about it. Now that Grandfather was gone, Susan was the *de facto* head of the family and he knew she had a strong reputation of her own to uphold long before that. Having it get around the upper circles that he was shirking his duty wouldn't do. It could cause Susan embarrassment. At any rate, he was glad Patty had tipped him off; she was cool like that.

Shortly after he got home and had a nice spaghetti Bolognese for dinner, he saw an e-mail from Deek in his in-box. The title was "Trouble." The e-mail went on to say that Tammy was fired from her counter job at CVS for several unannounced absences. Her drinking had escalated ("she spends more time in the company of Captain Morgan than she does me,") and her vomiting was so frequent now that Deek couldn't tell if it was due to the alcohol or her eating disorder. He was worried about her and miserable. Lately, Tammy was constantly going on about suing CVS for discriminating against her for having depression. Deek couldn't reason with her and she seemed to be a in a downward spiral. In desperation, he finally called her brother, who came over to check on her and wound up staying two days because he was too high to leave. Then the brother's drug-dealer, Rollo, came over to restock his supplies and keep the party going. The brother didn't have enough cash, so Deek had to pay Rollo. The e-mail concluded with Deek admitting that he was almost at his breaking point.

Almost? thought Bryce.

Deek closed by saying he'd call Bryce in a few days. Bryce sighed. What was it with him, he wondered, that made him so willing and able to take on women who were projects? Was it because he didn't get enough maternal attention, or because he was naturally kind-hearted, or because he just never seemed to click with normal women?

11

The following week found Bryce lunching with Aunt Bitsy. He'd picked her up at her house in New Rochelle. She had one of those real old-fashioned houses and she'd never done any updates, so it went from being frumpy to chic after about 40 years. When he knocked on the door, she answered it herself since it was Thursday, traditionally the maid's day off, and asked him to wait just a moment while she went upstairs to get her handbag. That was another one of those words he only heard around Aunt Bitsy.

He wandered around for a moment in her sunny sitting room and peered into the kitchen beyond. She had an enormous copper stove that Bryce found fascinating. He'd only ever seen one other at a house in New York City. Her husband had been a financier who had done very well for himself. They'd had a daughter about a decade older than Bryce named Pamela who was killed in a car accident in the Hamptons one summer in the 1970s. He remembered his mother helping Bitsy with the arrangements. Bitsy's husband had never gotten over it and died of a stroke a few years later. At the time, Mother had urged Bitsy to move to Tuxedo, but Bitsy's home was where she felt the most comfortable, so she'd stayed.

"I'm ready, dear," Aunt Bitsy cheerily announced, and Bryce helped her into his car. The New Rochelle Woman's Club wasn't far and she'd taken him there on a few occasions over the years. It reeked of old money and was filled with the kind of ladies that really were ladies; they never raised their voices, they were engaging when they spoke, and they devoted themselves tirelessly (or at least somewhat enthusiastically) to charitable causes. To Bryce, it felt like being in a giant hen-house with pastel walls and chintz curtains, but there was something comforting about it.

They arrived and were seated promptly. After some light banter with Aunt Bitsy, he was served assorted crudités and chicken salad (he simply had to order the chicken salad in a Woman's Club, not only because it was such a cliché, but because it was fantastic). Aunt Bitsy had the consommé and cream cheese sandwiches. She seemed slightly distracted and kept glancing at her watch, which was odd because they had no other appointments.

He soon found out why when Bitsy's eyes lit up and she hailed someone across the room.

"Why, it's Claudia!" she said, feigning what was obviously not surprise. "I had no idea she'd be here. Oh, Bryce, please let me introduce you."

Bryce stood up and turned to meet whomever it was that had caused Aunt Bitsy to give her best attempt at acting in aid of a matchmaking scheme. He saw a lovely brunette heading his way. She had a kindly smile and seemed happy to see Aunt Bitsy.

"Claudia, how nice to see you," Aunt Bitsy said. "Bryce, this is Claudia Burkle, the daughter of a good friend of Edward's." Edward was Aunt Bitsy's late husband.

"Pleased to meet you," Bryce said, shaking her hand.

"How do you do?" Claudia said, still smiling. The way her eyes crinkled at the corners gave him the impression she was stifling a snicker, probably because she was self-conscious at being part of this charade intended to bring them together.

Aunt Bitsy addressed Claudia. "Your mother is doing a magnificent job with the Program Committee; I chatted with her last week. Was she able to get the orchid man to speak?"

"Yes," Claudia replied.

Bryce conjured a mental image of Claudia's mother holding a dog biscuit aloft and commanding "Speak! Speak!" to a giant, mute half-man, half-orchid. Before he could pursue the thought, Aunt Bitsy turned to Bryce and explained "Claudia's mother's been trying for ages to get a local orchid expert to give us a talk about the care of orchids. We were afraid we were going to have to have the poinsettia lady in again this year if he couldn't make it."

"Oh, no; not the poinsettia lady!" Bryce said with mock horror. The ladies laughed lightly.

How significant everything in their world is, Bryce thought. Men weren't that particular, at least not about most things, but for women, the difference between a lecture about orchids and poinsettias was the difference between success and disaster. He remembered how exacting Mother was about which set of china should be used for which occasion, and how sharply she once upbraided a serving maid for using the wrong cocktail napkins. Their lives were a dizzying collage of details upon details, and everything had to be just right. No wonder they seemed to be under such pressure all the time, despite the serene veneer. He remembered Mother telling Susan "Be like the duck—above the surface, appear calm, but below the surface, paddle like hell." He was glad to be a man.

"Bryce is the son of my very dearest friend," Aunt Bitsy explained to Claudia, "And I know his mother would be terribly proud of him if she were still with us." She looked at Bryce wistfully when she said this. He knew she was still brokenhearted over Mother's death, probably even more than he was. She put her hand on his and he suddenly realized that her affection for him was more about him reminding her of Mother than it was about her appreciating him for who he actually was. He was Mother's ghost, he concluded, come to comfort Bitsy and relieve her loneliness with every gesture and facial expression that he'd inherited from her.

But it didn't matter. Bryce understood. She was a dear old woman.

“Claudia’s just returned from Prague, haven’t you?” Aunt Bitsy asked.

“From Vienna,” Claudia corrected.

Bryce wondered how anyone could mix up Prague and Vienna. Prague had to be the creepiest city on earth. There was something perpetually spooky about it, like the setting of an old horror film. He couldn’t stand the place, and figured people who lived there must have a constant case of the heebie-jeebies.

“Bryce has been to Vienna,” Aunt Bitsy offered, clearly trying to get him and Claudia talking.

“Lugano,” Bryce corrected. Aunt Bitsy was getting a globe for Christmas.

“Did you like it?” asked Claudia, trying to do her bit.

“Yes, it was very pleasant. I became a fondue addict,” he responded. The ladies laughed again.

“Is it really true that you should drink hot tea with fondue so the cheese doesn’t congeal in your stomach?” Claudia asked.

“I never noticed a difference when I didn’t,” he said, marveling at what a conversational reach she’d come up with.

Aunt Bitsy interjected. “You two have so much in common—it’s a shame you can’t discuss this at length.” She gave Bryce a look.

Claudia was pretty and at least she seemed intelligent. That was more than he could say for a lot of the girls Aunt Bitsy had introduced him to. “Would you care to have dinner with me sometime?”

Claudia seemed pleased. “That would be very nice. I’ll leave my contact information with Bitsy.”

With that, they said their goodbyes and Claudia departed, saying she was going to help her mother prepare for the orchid man’s lecture. Bryce was strangely gladdened as he beheld the scoop of chicken salad on his plate.

“Well done, dear,” Aunt Bitsy praised him. “Claudia is a lovely girl. Her father, Otto, was Edward’s best friend. He had several manufacturing plants in Europe. They’re very rich. You could do a lot worse, especially these days when so many families didn’t plan carefully and it starts to show. Otto was a very smart man.”

“Why doesn’t she have a boyfriend?” Bryce asked.

“She did. They were engaged until she found out about—” Aunt Bitsy did a sidelong glance and dropped her voice “*—the underwear.*”

Bryce could’ve pursued this intriguing statement but thought better of it; whatever perversion Claudia’s ex-fiancé engaged in, he was probably better off not knowing. Most of all, it was probably best not to hear it from someone Aunt Bitsy’s age. Out of a lifetime’s force of habit, she still whispered when she said the word "pregnant." At least she hadn't said "underpinnings." Bryce wouldn't have been able to contain his laughter if she had.

"Are you enjoying the dip for your crudités? I think it's the most delicious thing I've ever had. Believe it or not, I actually asked the cook what his recipe was, and you wouldn't believe the answer," Bitsy informed him. "It's just sour cream and that Hidden Valley Ranch powdered mix. Can you believe it?"

Bryce assured her he could not. He smiled and ate his chicken salad.

12

Aunt Bitsy had been dropped off back at home and promised Bryce she'd call him after Claudia called her with her phone number. She said that's the kind of thing she would normally already have, but these days with young people using cellphones, she was never sure what anyone's number was. (Aunt Bitsy longed for the bygone days of telephone exchanges.)

The next entry on his social calendar for the day was a visit with Rohan. He drove to Manhattan. Rohan lived on the Upper East Side but they were meeting at The Cloisters. Rohan was crazy about The Cloisters. It was always interesting to Bryce to know what kinds of things foreigners liked or disliked about America. Like how Cristina couldn't stand ice cubes in her drink, even on the hottest summer days.

They toured the latest exhibit and then sat on a bench in the gardens. The temperature was a bit bracing but it was very sunny. Rohan seemed a bit more reserved than usual, but he'd said he was tired from traveling. He'd returned from Boston only yesterday, having stayed longer than anticipated. He gave Bryce a pretend scowl.

"So tell me you haven't been seeing that crazy girl," he said admonishingly.

Bryce explained that Leslie had called after her drinking binge to tell him she'd picked someone up in the bar, but that she was getting back together with the married man.

Rohan shook his head. "Where did you meet this woman? In a psychiatric hospital?"

Bryce promised Rohan that he was done with Leslie even though he felt that it was a bit of a lie. He wasn't exactly done with her; he was just not as actively involved any more.

"Besides," he added, "Aunt Bitsy's set me up with some manufacturing heiress."

"Have you met her?" Rohan asked.

"Yes, just today at Aunt Bitsy's club. She's nice," Bryce remarked.

"Beautiful?" Rohan asked.

Bryce had to think for a moment. Claudia wasn't striking, but she was very attractive. "She's definitely good-looking," he said.

Rohan looked off into the distance and Bryce knew something was amiss. He would always do that when he was upset, stare off into the sky, as if he were expecting an airplane or something.

"Man, that's great," Rohan said. "You definitely want your woman to be good-looking, right?"

"Well, of course," Bryce answered, "But it's not just looks alone. There are other things."

"Like what?" Rohan asked. Bryce was surprised. This wasn't a typical Rohan conversation. Something was up.

"Well, you know, brains and good conversational skills and things like that," Bryce said.

Rohan looked back at Bryce and said "My family made a match for me." He didn't sound happy.

"That's great news," Bryce exclaimed, adding "Isn't it?"

"I don't know how to take this," Rohan said, awash with discouragement. "She's incredibly beautiful and she's from a very important family. They're filthy rich. They're dripping with money. My father says I'm the luckiest son alive. My mother is dancing with joy."

"So what's the problem?" asked Bryce.

"What's the problem?" Rohan said, loud enough that people nearby turned to look. "The problem is she's dumb as a bag of rocks! I'm telling you, this girl has no brains in her head. None! None at all!"

"You've met her?" Bryce asked.

"Yes, at a party; long ago. My parents don't even know about it. She's stupid, that's what I'm saying. Totally stupid."

"But she's beautiful and rich," Bryce reminded him. "Doesn't that make it any easier?"

"Look, how am I going to have a conversation with this woman? It's like trying to talk to a piece of wood!" Rohan complained.

"Well what about your horoscopes—don't they use those to make sure the two of you are a good match?" Bryce asked.

"The horoscopes came out perfectly, but the astrologer is still the old school. They think a wife should only be beautiful and a good hostess and things like that. It's rubbish. They don't consider I would ever want to discuss something or expect her to know things without my explaining everything," he argued. "Don't you understand? I don't want a stupid wife." He laughed his insane little laugh but it sounded sad.

Bryce didn't know what to say. He knew Rohan's father would be furious if he didn't marry this woman. They'd been trying to get him married for a while now and Rohan had successfully managed to evade capture, but at this point they were quite serious about settling him down, and the prospect of this rich bride was definitely a make-or-break deal. There probably wasn't any way Rohan could get out of it.

"Maybe she has other qualities. Some people aren't intellectual but they have heart. Is she very compassionate?" Bryce asked.

"I saw her kill a frog by stomping on it in high heels," Rohan said. Now he looked scared.

"That's disturbing," Bryce remarked. "What the hell kind of party was this, anyway?"

"A bunch of young people, we were having drinks," Rohan said.

"Was she drunk?" Bryce asked.

"No," Rohan said.

She's a sociopath, Bryce thought. He tried to come up with some kind of encouraging spin for that, but couldn't.

"Why do you think I'm completely knackered? I didn't sleep all night," Rohan said, hanging his head.

"You're a busy guy; you probably won't be spending that much time with her anyway, after you get married. She'll have her interests and you'll have yours," Bryce said in as comforting a tone as he could manage. "Look at Cristina—she and her husband don't see each other for months."

"But I don't want it to be like that," Rohan said. "Maybe I should move back to London. I won't tell my parents where I am."

"You can't do that," Bryce said.

"Sure I can," Rohan said, starting to laugh, "But then I'll run out of money and I'll have to open a curry house!" He clutched his stomach and he was giggling so hard he nearly fell off the bench.

Bryce got up and they started to walk.

"Or what about a chippy?" Rohan said enthusiastically. "Hey, you want some mushy peas with that?" he asked, before almost asphyxiating himself with hysterical laughter.

13

On Friday morning, Deek called.

"Tammy's gone," he said plaintively.

Bryce's gut reaction was that this news was cause for rejoicing, but he knew he couldn't express that to Deek. Instead, he was forced to take the "I'm sorry that you're sorry" tack that he always did when one of Deek's trashy girlfriends left.

"That's too bad. Did you two have a fight?" he asked.

"I'd had an evening out all planned for us and twenty minutes before we're supposed to leave, she's still not dressed, but she's got her things packed in boxes. I asked her what she was doing and she said she was leaving; that she couldn't take it any more," he explained.

"Couldn't take it?" Bryce repeated in astonishment. "Couldn't take what—the normal lifestyle, or you putting up with her constant drama?"

"That's the thing," Deek said in pained tones, "She said it was all my fault—that I put too much pressure on her. I made her miserable," he concluded.

"Deek, listen to me, that's not true. She made herself miserable," Bryce said sternly, adding, "And she made you miserable."

"That's not true," Deek protested. "I loved how sweet she could be, and how we'd talk for hours about things—"

Bryce cut him off. "Yes, like her catalogue of disorders."

"She wasn't that bad; hey, everyone has problems. But I miss her, and now I feel like I ruined her life," he said, sounding distraught.

Bryce paused a moment so what he was about to say would sink in, or at least he hoped it would. "Has it occurred to you yet how ironic it is that Tammy dumped you? A mentally unstable, uncultured, uneducated, delusional woman with a host of personal problems, all of her own making, decides that she needs to rid herself of a decent, honest guy way out of her league, who's done nothing but try to make her happy?"

There was silence as Deek tried to comprehend. "So you think the fact that things didn't work out is really her fault?"

"I don't think, I know," Bryce replied. "How many times have we had this conversation? I should just record it and play it back to you. You do this. You bring home stray women and think you can save them, but you can't. And do you know why you can't? It's not because you're not trying hard enough—it's because they do not want to be saved. They are miserable little people leading miserable little lives, and they like it that way. Everyone one of them winds up dragging you down with them."

"C'mon, that's not fair," Deek argued.

"Okay, then tell me this—has a single one of the women you've dated done anything supportive or helpful for you? Have they been there for you during a crisis? Have they brought anything good into your life? No. They have nothing to give. They take, and when they're done, they leave."

"So Tammy was planning this great heist all along, is that what you're saying? She went out with me so she could take things from me? You're wrong," Deek said.

"I'm not saying it's conscious," Bryce explained, "But they need things—attention, pity, drama—and you play along."

"I'm just trying to find a good relationship," Deek said. He sounded heartbroken.

“Stick with someone who isn’t so—different” Bryce chose his words carefully here; no use rubbing salt in Deek’s wound. “Aren’t there any women at the yacht club?” He knew Deek spent a lot of time there.

“Sure, but they’re all boring. They’re all the same,” he replied.

“Yes—*normal*. That’s what we’re shooting for,” Bryce said.

Bryce was not unsympathetic to Deek’s plight, but he was exhausted from years of helping him come to terms with breakup after breakup, only to see him dive into dangerous waters with utter abandon soon thereafter. Deek was a great guy and a true friend, and Bryce wished he were happy.

“I think the next woman you see should be a therapist,” Bryce offered, quickly adding, “I’m serious. You need help with this.”

Deek bristled. “No, I don’t do that therapy stuff. I’m just fine. I can take care of myself.”

“Talking to someone would give you insights into why you do things and help you find ways to get what you want out of life,” Bryce counseled.

“That’s what you’re for,” Deek responded. “I don’t need to pay some shrink to be my friend.”

Bryce thought of pushing the point but he knew it was no use. In some things, Deek had a stubborn southern streak that he couldn’t break. Like the time in college when Deek drank a whole bottle of Tabasco sauce because someone bet him he wasn’t man enough to do it. Bryce tried to tell him it was a stupid idea, but Deek would not be dissuaded. He was sick for days afterwards.

“Well,” Bryce said, “As your friend, I advise you to take it easy.”

“But Tammy’s gone,” Deek wailed.

“Yes, and so are all her imaginary illnesses and foul moods and crackhead relatives. You’ll finally be free; think of it that way,” Bryce said encouragingly.

“I’ll be alone,” Deek said, “But I’ll do my best.”

After they hung up, Bryce looked at his watch. He noted the time so he could keep track of how many hours it would be until Deek got mixed up with another mess of a girl.

13

Over the weekend Bryce thought of picking up some cashmere sweaters. His old ones were still in good shape but he wanted to buy a few extras for winter, especially since he’d be spending time at the cottage in Norfolk. It could get cold there in the country well into spring, especially in the evenings. That was the Berkshires for you. However, the thought of shopping on a weekend when everyone and their dog was hurriedly doing business during their two precious days off caused him to rethink. He’d go during a weekday.

Saturday night, he ordered a pizza for dinner.

"What name?" asked the person on the other end of the phone.

"Murphy," Bryce said. "M-U-R-P-H-Y."

"Got it. Fifteen minutes," the man said, and hung up.

Bryce always used "Murphy" when he ordered take-out or made reservations because not only did it save him from publicly revealing his surname (which he was taught never to do) but because everyone could spell it. Chinese, Lebanese, Italians, Greeks, Indians—nobody ever had trouble with that name. An old friend of his father's had tipped him off to the trick before he set off for college, and true enough, it worked like a charm.

He left his apartment and walked down the street, picked up the pizza, and was headed back when he saw Leslie approaching the door to his building.

He caught up to her in the lobby, saying "Hey, good to see you. Want some pizza?"

She turned to him with a pained look on her face. Bryce thought she looked exceptionally pale.

"I have food poisoning," she whispered.

Bryce wasn't sure why she'd come to his apartment in such a condition, but he bounded up the steps, unlocked the door, and ushered her in.

"Can I offer you some water? Maybe peppermint tea?" he added.

"Just water," she said, nodding appreciatively as she sat on the couch and pulled her coat down, exposing her shoulders but not entirely removing it.

Bryce set the pizza aside and brought her a glass of water, asking, "What happened?"

Leslie went on to explain—haltingly—that she'd gone out with Graham on Monday night. She'd ordered the seafood special: salmon encrusted with pistachios and herbs.

Bryce grimaced visibly, not even bothering to hide his reaction. Only a fool would order fish on a Monday—the chef's night off. It was probably purchased on Friday and encrusted on Monday to hide a weekend's worth of decomposition.

Leslie said they had a terrible fight during the meal, in sharp contrast to the prior weeks, which she reported were blissful until she found out he had continued sleeping with Romy. There at the table, she confronted him, thinking that doing so in a romantic setting might compel him to propose. Instead, he became furious at her for spying on him and informed her he'd been cheating on her with someone else even before Romy. He stalked out of the restaurant, leaving Leslie with the bill.

She decided to take the fish with her, partly because she was in a daze and partly because it was expensive and she felt she should keep it since she paid for it. It sat in her refrigerator until Thursday night, when she was hungry after three days of mourning the relationship and trying unsuccessfully to contact Graham. Bryce suspected it was something of a death-wish that led her to eat the fish, and from there it was only a matter of time before she was in an excruciating state of digestive distress. She'd been violently ill since then and only now felt the need to get out of her apartment and seek the comfort of a sympathetic listener.

Bryce cocked his head to one side and tried to figure out what was wrong with Leslie and what was wrong with him for putting up with it. She was chasing something unattainable, oblivious to the personal cost. She was actually moving in a direction opposite her goal; if she wanted to better herself, there were nonprofit boards he could've helped her join and charity circles to which he could've introduced her. She could spend her free time learning a second language (she didn't even speak one) or cultivating an interesting hobby. In time, her social capital would rise as a natural progression. It was clear to Bryce that she didn't understand the nature of what she was striving for, and sadly, there was no way he could explain it to her in a way she could comprehend.

As for himself, he realized with stunning clarity that Leslie was a lost cause he'd deluded himself into thinking he could rescue. She was never going to listen to him. She would never be grateful. He was wasting his time.

Suddenly he was sick of her. The terrier-dog cuteness about her had been irreparably tainted by her delusional dreams, repulsive behavior, and abject stupidity. She was destined to spend the rest of her life trying to get flashy rich poltroons to adore her and then engaging in self-destructive acts when they didn't. It was a never-ending cycle of torture that filled some very deep need within her that self-respect and the sincere affection of a good man would never do.

His mind turned briefly to Claudia. They were meeting for dinner Tuesday.

Leslie interrupted his thought by asking quietly "Do you think there's any hope for us?"

Bryce sighed and sat forward. He put his hands on hers. "I'm afraid not. I don't think we're enough alike, to be honest."

Leslie jumped off the couch, her wayward coat-sleeve swinging behind her to knock a small statue off Bryce's end-table and send it crashing to the hardwood floor.

"Not *you*," she intoned derisively, "Graham and I!"

Bryce simply shook his head. He rose and went to the door, opening it.

"Leslie, go home," he said. "You need rest. Go home."

Leslie stormed out, and Bryce said "Drink plenty of fluids," as she passed him.

He closed the door, looking at the shattered statue. *She didn't even apologize for breaking it*, he thought. He knew she couldn't afford to replace it, but he reasoned she could've apologized anyway. But that was the way his kind of people did things.

14

On the way to pick up Claudia, Bryce shivered and realized winter had definitely arrived.

By the time they'd been seated at the restaurant, they'd barely spoken. Claudia wasn't particularly chatty, and Bryce for some reason wasn't in his usual conversant mood. He remembered reading that everyone has about 40 hours of conversation in them and realized he'd used very little thus far. He wasn't sure if this were a good thing or not.

After he'd ordered the wine, Claudia said "Aunt Bitsy told me you had a varied professional life."

"Figures she would sum it up that way," Bryce responded, smiling. "She looks like a boxy old woman, but she has formidable diplomatic skills."

"I don't think of her as boxy," Claudia said, raising an eyebrow.

For some reason, his excitement about seeing her was fading. She wasn't turning out to be as much fun as he hoped.

"I just meant she . . . I don't know what I meant," he concluded, shrugging.

"So what kinds of things did you do?" Claudia continued. She was remaining on point, Bryce observed. Good hunter.

He explained his work as a writer at different companies and his teaching stint, summing it up by saying "So that's my collective wreck of a past." Claudia didn't laugh. She didn't even grin.

"I work with an arts council; we distribute grants," she explained. She gave a lengthy description of the foundation for which she worked. Bryce thought the whole thing sounded pretty bloated, but kept his opinion to himself.

Their talk turned to real estate, and Bryce's new holdings. Claudia owned some apartments in the area that she was thinking of selling.

"I should probably call Octavia L. Bell," she concluded.

Octavia L. Bell's real estate empire had been a staple in the county for decades. Bryce went to school with one of Bell's grand-nephews. He was kind of empty-headed, but likeable. Once, at a childhood birthday party for the lad, which Bryce had attended, Octavia L. Bell made a grand appearance to drop off a birthday card, which probably contained a massive check, he realized in hindsight. She had an air of superiority around her that was so strong it was as odorous as her extravagant perfume.

"Octavia L. Bell is a pompous old broad," he quipped. Claudia's face registered instant shock. *She really doesn't have a sense of humor*, he thought to himself.

"Octavia L. Bell is an expert at high-end real estate. Her personal and professional reputation are absolutely beyond question, or I wouldn't even consider engaging her services for this sale," Claudia informed him.

"I'm sorry," Bryce said. "I didn't mean anything against her. It's just that I met her once and she was a very stiff character."

"Not everyone is a comedian," Claudia said flatly.

You're telling me, he thought.

He continued "I'm sure she's very capable at what she does. I know she's very highly respected."

At that moment, their dinner was served, and by some unspoken mutual consent, the conversation took a lighter turn: travel, literature, and the scourge of Dutch elm disease in New York and Connecticut.

Before she alighted from his car when he dropped her off at home, he asked if she'd like to go out again. She surprised him by saying yes. She gave him an air kiss on one cheek and said goodnight. He closed the car door and headed around to the driver's side, genuinely stunned by her acceptance.

As he drove home, he tried imagining her reaction when she discovered her ex-fiancé's mysterious underwear perversion. He laughed out loud.

15

The time between early December and the holidays fairly flew by. Before he knew it, Bryce was contemplating Christmas. In the weeks leading up to it, he and Claudia saw each other three more times, and he and Aunt Bitsy had gone to the city to see *The Fantasticks*.

"Oh, that was simply *magnificent*," she raved as they left the theatre. He was touched that he could bring her so much joy, but still incredulous that anyone could find such drivel even tolerable. He knew "Soon It's Gonna Rain" would be stuck in his head for weeks.

Aunt Bitsy also made sure to get a reading on how things were going between him and Claudia on the way home, which he freely offered up, knowing it would be no use to attempt evasion. He explained that they were somewhat comfortable together, which was about the most charitable thing he could say. He didn't dislike Claudia, but while he found her attractive and willing, he didn't necessarily have any strong feelings towards her, either.

"Bryce," Aunt Bitsy had said a long moment after his update, "You know that those breathless romances you see in the movies aren't real. I forgot who said it, but someone once described a good marriage as two people running a small but boring non-profit, and that's exactly what it is. It's about having the correct priorities and caring for one another; being polite, being understanding. So many young men these days are dissatisfied with lovely girls from good homes because they harbor some immature fantasy that they'll marry someone who looks like a model and expresses endless interest in their hobbies and dreams, but it's just not like that. You will always be two individuals. It's the mutual respect that keeps you together. Do you understand what I'm saying?"

"Yes, Aunt Bitsy," Bryce replied.

"Your mother worried about your prospects; I think you're mature enough now that I can share that with you," she added.

"She worried about me? Why?" asked Bryce, concerned.

"Because she knew you were the kind of man who had his head in the clouds. She worried that you wouldn't be sensible when it came time to marry, and she didn't want to see you throwing yourself away on a *mésalliance* that wouldn't make you happy," she explained frankly.

So Mother had foreseen that Bryce would get mixed up with someone like Leslie. He realized he'd matured enough to avoid that kind of entanglement, but he still didn't know how to move forward with the right partner. As if clairvoyant, Aunt Bitsy addressed that dilemma.

"Claudia is a quality young woman from a good family. She's intelligent and has a gracious way about her. She would be a very pleasant and stable wife and a good mother. She's not flighty or self-absorbed. She would make a good partner for you—a good balance to your own personality," she stated.

Is she suggesting I'm flighty and self-absorbed? Bryce wondered.

"If you want to know the truth, I think that Claudia intended to marry that other man until—" she broke off, giving Bryce a look. "Have you stopped to consider that she may have had her hopes dashed, and that she finds herself alone now and wishing she could have a family before it's too late?"

Bryce had to admit he hadn't thought of Claudia as being vulnerable; she seemed to have her act completely together. She came off as utterly self-sufficient and content. But hearing Aunt Bitsy say that, he felt a pang of sadness, imagining her as privately feeling lonely and facing a biological clock that was running out of time.

"This is the kind of situation where two people who come together can become more than the sum of their parts," she explained. "Don't you remember that scene in 'It's a Wonderful Life' where George finds Mary in that alternate existence where he was never born, and she's a sad old spinster? But in the real-life part of the film, they're married and have a lively home filled with children?"

Apparently, Aunt Bitsy's appetite for bad holiday fare included that old dog of a movie, too, thought Bryce. He realized she was picturing him as George, an inept, mentally unstable blockhead, and Claudia as Mary, a beautiful woman who was pathologically devoted to him while gleefully raising their litter of children. It was an unsettling comparison.

He also surmised that Aunt Bitsy's emphasis on procreation was probably due to the fact that her only child was dead, and parenthood had taken on an obsessive, idealized quality in her grief-stricken mind. Not that Bryce was against having children someday, but he didn't necessarily think of it as a goal.

"The holidays are coming up," Aunt Bitsy said with a slight smile. Bryce waited for the rest of the sentence, but it never came. Then it hit him: she was suggesting he propose.

"Are you saying I should ask Claudia to marry me?"

"I think it would be a very wise idea," she said. "In fact, I think it's exactly what your mother would say if she were here right now," adding with emphasis, "I'm quite certain it's what she would say."

Aunt Bitsy was a conniver and a diplomatic arranger, but she was never outright or obvious. That she would put forth such an idea so boldly and forcefully made Bryce think he'd been missing a lot more subtle hints along the way than even he had guessed.

"If you like, I can go along with you to help you choose a ring," she offered. "It needn't be anything extravagant—don't worry—but it should be the right kind of stone."

Bryce thought a moment and shakily said, "Well, you don't have to; I mean, I can always ask Patty."

"Oh dear, no," Aunt Bitsy countered. "Knowing her, she'd pick something that looked like Picasso designed it. You know I think she's very sweet, but her tastes are too *outré* for a mission like this." She leaned towards Bryce and lowered her voice. "She's also a bit on the spendy side, I hate to tell you. Susan's had to have some talks with her about budget."

Aunt Bitsy left Bryce with a promise to get back to him about good dates for ring-shopping. After she was gone, Bryce felt disoriented. He was going to marry Claudia, just like that. He kept seeing James Stewart in his mind, running through the snow. It didn't go at all with "Soon It's Gonna Rain."

16

"Brother, have I found a winner this time!" exclaimed Deek.

Bryce pulled the phone away from his ear and looked at it for a moment. It had only been a couple of weeks since the demise of Whatever Her Name Was. He put the phone back alongside his head and said "That's great news, Deek."

Clearly he hadn't feigned excitement convincingly enough because Deek said "Listen, I know what you're thinking but I want you to know that I really thought long and hard about your advice last time we talked. You said I needed to shoot for normal, and that's what I did."

"So this one is normal?" Bryce asked skeptically.

Deek laughed. "Yes, Tiffany's definitely normal."

Tiffany? thought Bryce. *What did they name her brother, T.J.Maxx?*

"Let me guess—you met her at the yacht club," Bryce offered.

Deek guffawed. "No, she's not like that. We met in a bar."

Smashing. She passed out and he brought her home.

"You'll never guess what happened," Deek happily taunted.

"I'll bet I can," Bryce retorted.

"I passed out and she brought me home!"

That's a first, thought Bryce.

"Yeah, she says I'm an idiot, don't you darling?"

At that point he heard Deek's laughter and a scuffle in the background, and then Deek said "Here, say hello to my new sweetheart."

Bryce hated when people did that. He wasn't even aware that their conversation wasn't private, and now he was having some misbegotten bar-fly shoved in his face. She spoke.

"Hey," was all she said. Bryce felt certain he could detect the sound of gum-chewing.

"Hi there, I'm Bryce."

"Yeah, Deek told me all about you two. You know, your friend's a complete moron," she said matter-of-factly.

"He has his moments," Bryce said, but he was insulted she would talk that way about him.

"If I hadn't taken him home, they woulda called the cops," she explained.

What does she want, a medal? Is this her way of saying she found him irresistible?

"Well, it was very nice of you to do that," Bryce remarked.

"Hell yeah," she said, adding "Most guys like that, I don't give the time of day."

One would hope not, Bryce thought, wondering exactly how much of her time she spent in bars until closing.

"He looked okay," she conceded, then immediately said "So, are you as smart as Deek says?"

"Deek says I'm smart?" he asked.

"Yeah. He says you're the smartest person he knows," she said.

"I don't know if I'd go that far," Bryce replied. He was about to make a dumb joke about being smart enough to know how stupid he was when she interrupted.

"Because most of you rich guys are dumb as a bag of rocks," she said.

Oh, great. So she's going to do the "rich guys" thing, Bryce thought. For Deek's sake, he tried to be congenial.

"A lot of guys have more dollars than brains, I won't argue with you on that one."

"Well, Deek says you got a lotta dollars," she said pointedly.

“Yes, well, Deek would know,” he shot back, hoping he could end the call. Deek must’ve read his mind because he heard him in the background affectionately saying “Here, Darling, let me get back on the line. Don’t want my friend stealing you away from me.”

Faintly he could hear Tiffany in the background saying “Fat chance.”

“Isn’t she something?” Deek asked delightedly.

“Yes, she is,” Bryce replied.

“What about you, fella? What’s going on with you?” Deek asked.

“The renovations are finished at the cottage in Norfolk,” Bryce reported.

“The roof and everything?” Deek asked.

“Yes,” Bryce said. He started saying something about the contractor when he heard loud sounds in the background, as if someone were rummaging around. He could hear Tiffany shouting “Where the fuck is the remote?” He had planned to mention the latest with Claudia but he realized Deek was distracted.

“Listen, Deek, I should go,” Bryce said.

“Sure thing, Bryce—we’ll catch up later.”

Before he hung up, Bryce heard Deek saying to Tiffany, “Now don’t get all upset—it’s here somewhere,” as Tiffany released a string of expletives.

The idea of Claudia seemed better and better by the moment. At least he’d never have to be embarrassed by her. Then he had a terrible thought: eventually, he and Deek and Claudia and Tiffany would have to get along socially. He couldn’t even imagine introducing Claudia to someone like Tiffany. He could never do that to her. He resolved that he’d have to tell Deek a preliminary fib about Claudia having migraines or something so he could believably use it as an excuse to get out of joining them when the occasion arose.

“If you’re going to lie, lie well,” Grandfather used to say.

17

Bryce was feeling claustrophobic in the small jeweler’s shop. Maybe it was because he and Aunt Bitsy had their heavy coats on, which made everything seem stuffy.

“What exactly am I supposed to be looking for?” Bryce asked.

“That’s what Mr. Benetto is here for,” Aunt Bitsy said. “Isn’t that right, Mr. Benetto?”

“That’s absolutely right. Your aunt tells me you need a very special engagement ring for a very special girl. I have some beautiful options all prepared. All you have to do is tell me which one you think says ‘I love you’ just the right way,” he explained.

Aunt Bitsy made a little sound of approval. “Oh, isn’t that sweet? See? This is going to be easy.”

But what if I don't want to say 'I love you'? he wondered.

Mr. Benetto waved him over to the well-lit counter before him where a tray with five rings was ready for Bryce's consideration. They were all platinum but the diamond shapes were different, round, square, oval, and two that had some extra smaller diamonds on the sides. Bryce felt like he was standing on stage, the light from above was so bright.

"How much is this one?" Bryce asked, picking up the plain square-cut diamond ring.

Mr. Benetto remained silent as he and Aunt Bitsy exchanged looks. Aunt Bitsy quickly said "These are all in your range. Is that the one you prefer?"

Bryce moved it around in the light. It looked okay.

"I suppose so," Bryce replied.

He handed the ring to Mr. Benetto and for a moment, their eyes met. In a flash, he knew that Mr. Benetto knew that he didn't really want this ring because he didn't really want the woman that went with it. This wasn't the first time Mr. Benetto had sold an engagement ring. Bryce wished he could talk to someone like Mr. Benetto, who was about the age his father would've been were he still alive; not that his father would've had any great advice, but he felt he needed the counsel of an older and more experienced man. Mr. Benetto looked like he had plenty of experience.

"Is it returnable?" Bryce asked while Mr. Benetto boxed the ring.

"Bryce!" Aunt Bitsy exclaimed.

"I mean in case she doesn't like it," Bryce explained.

"She'll like it," Aunt Bitsy snapped.

She and Mr. Benetto chatted for a moment about a brooch she was admiring; they'd known each other a long time.

"This will be one Christmas that Claudia will never forget," Aunt Bitsy said happily.

"Actually, I thought I'd wait until New Year's," Bryce said.

"You're not going to get engaged for Christmas?" she said with obvious disappointment.

"It's just that there are already so many gifts," Bryce suggested.

"An engagement ring is *not* a regular gift," Aunt Bitsy said.

"But if everyone expects to get engaged for Christmas, it'll make it that much more surprising if I wait until New Year's," Bryce said.

After the ring had been rung up, Mr. Benetto handed it to Bryce along with the receipt.

"In case she changes her mind," he said quietly.

18

Going to Susan's for Christmas was something Bryce looked forward to all year. This would be the first Christmas without Grandfather, but for some reason, Bryce didn't think that should make things more somber. On the contrary, he felt more effusively happy than ever. Maybe it was because he wanted to celebrate Grandfather's life rather than mourn his loss, or maybe because the old man had a way of creating a stifling presence in his midst that would be absent this year. In any event, Bryce was brimming with holiday spirit when he pulled into Tuxedo Park. As he walked towards the house, Patty ran out to greet him.

"Welcome to Christmas at the Robinson-Parnells!" she called out, embracing him. "We've missed you," she said as she hugged his arm and gave him a big kiss on the cheek.

"Get in here and close that door," Susan said from within. "You'll catch a chill and all the heat is going out."

Patty looked sheepishly at Bryce and they both giggled as they walked inside.

Susan and Patty were expecting a small group for dinner that afternoon. Uncle Clement, who was Grandfather's brother, and his wife, Fluff, would be there. Aris Jorgensen and his wife Loretta were also coming; they were in-laws of his mother's deceased step-brother. At this point, they weren't technically relatives, but they'd been in-laws so long, they'd become family, even if the ties that connected them had since dissolved. Their longtime neighbors, Minty and Ingrid Masterson, would be there, along with their daughter, Nathalie, and her new fiancé. Rounding out the guest list would be Monsignor Ryan and his wife, Marguerite.

Susan and Patty had spent Christmas Eve with Patty's family in King of Prussia.

"Did you have a nice time?" Bryce asked when he came down for cocktails. Margaret's son John, who was on winter break from Fordham, had helped him carry his bags upstairs. He was glad of the help because he had brought a lot of presents and he didn't want to put them under the tree until later.

"Very nice," Susan reported. "Patty's dad is having an extension put on the garage. They're doing a good job."

"You know how those old Victorian houses are," Patty explained. "They just got sick of never having enough room for all the cars, especially when my brothers are over." Patty had three brothers.

"Maybe that's something we should think about," Susan said, looking in Patty's direction.

Patty shrugged. "I don't mind parking in the driveway if we have guests," she said.

"Speaking of," Susan said, "You'll get to meet Nathalie Masterson's fiancé."

"Oh, right; I heard something about that," Bryce replied.

"Big Chinese money. *Big* money," Susan said, clearly impressed. It took a lot of money to impress Susan, so the guy must have been rolling in it.

"His name is Bingwen and he met Nathalie in Switzerland early last year at a work seminar," Patty said.

Nathalie and Bryce were friends. She was much younger, but once she reached her late teens they found themselves being invited to the same parties and began to hang out together occasionally.

"I don't know why the hell you didn't go out with Nathalie when you had the chance. Do you know how much money Minty has?" Susan asked.

Patty intervened. "I don't think it's fair to talk about what Bryce should or shouldn't have done. It's Christmas. We're supposed to be celebrating."

"Yes, but he'd really have something to celebrate if he had Minty's money," Susan quipped, unwrapping a colorfully wrapped chocolate from a bowl on the end-table and popping it into her mouth.

Patty smiled at him and said, "Bryce, I hope you don't think I'm prying, but Aunt Bitsy told us you've been seeing Claudia Burkle and that it's getting serious."

"Yes, sort of," he said. A disturbing look of surprise registered simultaneously in both Patty's and Susan's eyes, so he deduced Aunt Bitsy had told them about the ring-shopping. "I mean, nothing is definite yet until we talk about it, but we may be making plans for the future." He tried to smile in a casual yet nervous way, hoping they would read it as pre-proposal jitters lest Claudia turn him down.

They apparently bought it, because they both assured him that she would accept, and praised him on his choice.

"I haven't met her, but I know people who have, and they speak of her with great respect," Patty said sweetly. Bryce figured she had already chosen the dress she was going to wear to the wedding.

"I like her, Bryce," said Susan. "She's not flighty like you. You need someone like her."

This was the second time in recent memory that he'd been called "flighty." Did people really think of him that way?

Bryce heard an almost inaudible cough to his far right. It was Margaret, standing in the doorway, being her usual discreet-yet-pervasive self.

"Would you like John to bring down the presents now?" she asked Bryce.

Before he could answer, Susan said "We'll open them after our guests leave. Thank you, Margaret."

"Yes Ma'am," said Margaret, and with that, she vanished into the kitchen.

"John's doing very well," Susan remarked.

"Is he?" said Bryce. "Good for him."

The doorbell rang and moments later, Margaret showed Monsignor Ryan and his wife into the living room.

"Susan! Patty!" cried Marguerite Ryan, greeting them, while Bryce shook Monsignor Ryan's hand.

"Merry Christmas, Mr. Ryan," Bryce said.

"Stop being so formal. You can call me Ned," Monsignor Ryan instructed with a smile.

Monsignor Ryan had been a friend of his father's. He and Marguerite were Catholics, and Monsignor Ryan was something of a character. One night, he and his father and some others had gone out to dinner. When the waiter brought the check, Monsignor Ryan asked "Do you offer a clergy discount?"

Assuming he must be a clergy member to be asking the question, the waiter said "Yes, just a moment," and went and recalculated the bill. After that, his father and the others started calling him "Monsignor," to the point that most people actually believed he was one.

Calling him by his given name seemed strange to Bryce since his whole life he'd heard him referred to as "Monsignor Ryan" or simply "the Monsignor."

The Ryans had just settled in when the doorbell rang again. This time it was Uncle Clement and Aunt Fluff.

Uncle Clement was a slightly younger and slightly less fierce version of Grandfather. He was getting on in years and Bryce could tell that losing Grandfather this year had been hard. He'd been meaning to visit him but had never gotten around to it, mostly because he didn't like Aunt Fluff.

Aunt Fluff was nice in general, but she could be horrifically disrespectful in a way that most people of her generation had long since overcome. Nothing she said was ever mean-spirited, but Bryce realized if anyone outside their circle ever heard the things she said, they'd be shocked.

The two of them had an air of stodginess about them and they habitually wore wan smiles. With the right wardrobe, they could've been mistaken for a pair of garden gnomes.

"Clement," Aunt Fluff was saying, "You should sit by the fire." She turned to Bryce, and quietly said "He hasn't been himself lately. Woodrow's death has made him think about his own mortality. I'm at my wit's end to keep him in a cheerful mood." Bryce didn't find that difficult to believe.

Monsignor Ryan greeted Uncle Clement after he'd made himself comfortable in one of the big leather chairs beside the fireplace. Bryce could tell that Uncle Clement wasn't particularly thrilled to have Catholics in the house for a family celebration, but he made a vague attempt to hide it in the spirit of the holidays.

Marguerite Ryan and Bryce were having a nice conversation about the town of Norfolk. One of Marguerite's longtime friends had grown up there. Soon, Bryce found himself unable to hear her. He could see her lips move, but all he could hear was something very loud and powerful from the foyer.

Minty Masterson had arrived. In true form, he was laughing and greeting Susan and Patty in his booming voice. There was no such thing as Minty making a subtle entrance. In tow were Ingrid, Nathalie, and a handsome Asian man Bryce figured was the fiancé. He looked about ten years younger than Bryce and he was in fantastic shape. The suit he was wearing was understated, but it probably cost more than Bryce earned in a year when he was teaching.

So this is what big Chinese money looks like up close, he thought.

He walked over to greet Nathalie.

"Bryce! Hi!" she squealed, giving him a peck on the cheek. Nathalie was very sweet. She was the kind of girl you could describe as simple, but she was simple in a good way. She had a certain innocence about her that was extremely charming. Minty and Ingrid had seen to it that she led a very sheltered life. In her soft pink cashmere sweater-dress and wearing a delicate string of pearls around her neck, Bryce thought she could pass for a Christmas angel, fit for the top of a tree.

Ingrid stepped in. "Bryce, I'd like to introduce you to Bingwen Lu, our future son-in-law."

Shouldn't this be the other way around? thought Bryce. *Shouldn't she be introducing him to me? I'm not the newcomer.*

"Pleased to meet you, Bryce," said the man, extending his hand. "You can call me Ben."

"But do you know what I call him?" Minty boomed. "I call him Bing, like Bing Crosby! He even resembles him, doesn't he?" Minty was jovial. There were a few polite snickers to acknowledge the joke.

"It's so nice of your sister to invite us for Christmas," Ben said. "Nathalie has told me so much about your family."

"We're so pleased to have you, Ben," said Patty, rushing over to embrace him.

"We're so proud of him," said Ingrid, beaming at Bryce. Bryce thought for a moment that he caught a certain smugness in Ingrid's tone, but he figured he must be mistaken.

Bryce had always been a special favorite of Ingrid. She had a way of fawning over him that was certainly an ego-boost. His mother had never been the fawning type, but Ingrid did it in a way that wasn't cloying, just flattering. This made it all the more surprising that she didn't really greet him, but passed through into the living room to say hello to Uncle Clement and Aunt Fluff without so much as a word to him. Probably she wanted to be supportive to Uncle Clement in light of his recent bereavement. That must be it.

"Bryce!" Minty said, intoning his name so loudly the shock nearly knocked him over. Minty had a painfully firm handshake. Bryce always forgot that until it was too late.

"You're a man to be reckoned with now, aren't you?" he said, referring to Bryce's inheritance. Minty loved to talk about money. Bryce imagined that's where he got his nickname.

Before Bryce could answer, Minty told him that he had some good investment opportunities courtesy of his future son-in-law which were worth considering. Minty patted him on the back so hard he coughed involuntarily.

"Thanks, Minty," said Bryce, choking a bit. He realized that his hand was still throbbing. "I'll definitely think about it."

"A lot of things are opening up now in China," Minty explained, excitedly. "The sleeping giant has awoken!" He spread his arms wide, as if to greet the giant.

Bryce was spared a bombastic lesson in Chinese investments by the arrival of Aris and Loretta Jorgensen. Aris was the polar opposite of Minty. He was a soft-spoken, staid intellectual. Loretta was the retired dean of a Seven Sisters college.

After greeting everyone, Aris and Loretta entrenched themselves at Ben's side. They were eager learners and loved all things cultural, so they were engrossed in everything Ben had to say about China.

Meanwhile, from where he was standing, Bryce overheard a bit of Aunt Fluff's conversation with Monsignor Ryan.

"Well, nowadays we have to think of the coloreds," she was saying.

Lest he be pulled into the gravitational orbit of that discussion, he moved in Ingrid's direction, hoping for a bit of friendly adoration, but she merely gave a tight smile and walked past him to Ben, offering to have Margaret refresh his drink. She put her arm lightly around Ben as he chatted with Aris and Loretta, and it seemed to Bryce again that she cast her eyes in his direction with some shade of malice. He was sure he wasn't imagining it this time.

"This could've been you," he read in her cool gaze.

He felt displaced. Everyone was making much over Ben. That little family circle had closed up neatly now that it had all its components and Bryce was the outsider. He realized his former status with the Mastersons had been preponderant upon the expectation that he would marry Nathalie. It stung him to see Ingrid fussing over Ben, and even more to see Minty chatting with him in that father-son way that he used to do with him.

He reasoned he'd never given the Mastersons false hopes about his intentions with Nathalie. He and Nathalie were always friends and had spent time together over the years going to the cinema, going out for ice cream, playing Scrabble, or occasionally being each other's escorts for formal functions, but it had been strictly platonic. Now Ingrid looked like she'd bite Bryce if he came too close to Nathalie, she was that protective of Ben's claim on her daughter. Everything about the situation made Bryce feel diminished at a time when, for the first Christmas ever, he was a landed gentleman in his own right.

Bryce had another drink. Christmas was becoming depressing. He wanted to engage in pleasant chit-chat. He noticed Marguerite Ryan returning to the living room and approached her to finish their conversation about Norfolk that had been interrupted by the Masterson's arrival.

"You were telling me about your friend," he began, but Marguerite explained that she was on her way into the kitchen with a phone number for John. It was some contact of hers who might be of assistance to him in finding a summer job.

Now Bryce really felt like the odd man out. The Mastersons and Jorgensens were locked in Ben's enthrall and Marguerite was helping John qualify for the Horatio Alger Award.

"Bryce, dear," Aunt Fluff said, as if on cue. "Come over and tell us all about yourself. What are you up to these days?"

Bryce turned and walked towards Aunt Fluff, hoping his expression masked the apprehension he was feeling.

"Well, I've been busy fixing up Grandfather's cabin in Norfolk, and making decisions about investments," he reported.

Aunt Fluff smiled her wan smile. She reached out her bony hand, adorned with several large-carat diamond rings, and drew him close to her. She smelled of powder that was masking the scent of something that faintly resembled rotting fruit and ammonia.

"Now, we've heard that you may be announcing an engagement very soon," she said brightly.

What did Aunt Bitsy do, notify everyone on the planet? thought Bryce.

"Otto Burkle's daughter, is that right?" Uncle Clement asked. Bryce couldn't tell from his tone whether he approved or disapproved. He had Grandfather's knack for saying things in such a way that you weren't sure if you were in trouble or about to be congratulated.

"Yes, Claudia Burkle," Bryce replied.

Aunt Fluff sat back and beamed. "Oh, well, that's nice, isn't it, Clement?" she said, turning to Uncle Clement.

"Nothing is final yet, of course, but I'm planning to ask her soon," Bryce clarified.

"Otto did very well for himself," Uncle Clement explained. "Manufacturing. He had several plants in Europe. Your grandfather wanted to go into business with him in Canada but Otto wasn't interested in Canada. He loved it over there. Died over there, I think, didn't he?"

"Yes. In Vienna, I think," Bryce said.

"Nice place to die," Uncle Clement said pensively.

"But what about the two of you?" Aunt Fluff asked, changing the subject. "Where will you be making your home together?"

"We really haven't got that far, Aunt Fluff. We've only known each other a few months," Bryce explained.

"You'll have your whole lives to sort out the details," Uncle Clement said. "Fluff's a typical woman—wants to know what color the curtains will be."

"That's not so, Clement, I'm just inquiring. So many young people nowadays are relocating. My sister's daughter and her husband settled in McLean, Virginia. He's a diplomat. A lot of them live there and she tells me it's a very nice enclave—you know—but I don't see how they do without the cultural benefits that we have up here. Her children are going to grow up to be hillbillies, I think," said Aunt Fluff.

"Not going to that fifteen-thousand-dollar-a-year private school, they're not," countered Uncle Clement.

"That's another thing," said Aunt Fluff. "I don't see how they command those prices. I really don't. It's not Groton."

"No, it's not," said Uncle Clement. "Groton is fifty thousand." Like Grandfather, Uncle Clement knew the price of everything. You could mention anything in the world—rent on a 5,000-square-foot warehouse in Lawrence, Kansas; the price of a ton of soybeans in Cairo; annual dues for an obscure golf club in the Hebrides—and he'd come up with a figure that was pretty damn accurate. If Uncle Clement ever fell on hard times, Bryce figured he could always market his astounding ability as a lucrative lounge act, taking questions from the audience and having an assistant verify his answers online.

"All I'm saying is that you should think carefully about where you choose to live. All this spreading out is also spreading us thin," Aunt Fluff said.

Bryce was about to assure her that he'd stay in the northeast when one of Minty's humorous stories became so loud, everyone had to stop talking and turned to listen.

Minty's tale was in progress: "So the salesgirls go into his office in a panic and they tell him that by the time they realized that nobody had gotten her name, she'd already left with the mink coat. All she'd said was 'Charge it to my account,' but they had absolutely no idea whose account to charge it to. So he thinks it over for a moment and asks them a few questions: What color hair did she have? Was she tall and slender or short and petite? What sort of figure did she have? Then, once he had their answers, he told them to leave and not to worry about it, that he'd take care of it. You see, he knew the mistresses of all the big-shots in Dallas, and since he knew what kind of women their tastes ran to, he narrowed it down to ten millionaires whom this woman might've been the mistress of. So he sent an invoice for the fur coat to each of the ten guys, and within the week, he got back eight checks!"

Everyone roared with laughter. Minty met all kinds of powerful figures in his travels and he always had amusing stories to tell about them.

Just as Bryce was about to find a reason to excuse himself from Aunt Fluff's company, Margaret announced that dinner was being served.

At the table, Bryce found that Susan had seated him between Loretta Jorgensen and the Monsignor. Susan sat at the head of the table with Patty opposite at the far end. Nathalie and Ben were down near Patty; Uncle Clement and Aunt Fluff were seated by Susan, who, Bryce acknowledged, had infinitely more patience with them than he did. He found it odd that while Susan was impatient and demanding much of the time, she seemed to have infinite tolerance for annoying old people. Maybe years of being close to Grandfather had caused it. He wasn't sure.

Minty was clanging a fork against a glass to get everyone's attention, as if his loud voice wasn't enough.

He said "I'd like everyone to know that tonight is the first official announcement of my daughter Nathalie's engagement to Mr. Bing Crosby!" Everyone laughed lightly and Margaret stood at the ready with the bottle of champagne if extra were needed.

Minty continued. "I'd like everyone to raise their glasses as I toast the happy couple. Nathalie, your mother and I love you very much and we're very proud of you. You'll always be my little girl. Bing, I never thought I would know the joy of having a son, but that's what you are to me. Ingrid and I wish you both all the health and happiness in the world. To Nathalie and Bing!"

"Nathalie and Bing!" repeated the guests, and everyone sipped their champagne. Bryce emptied his glass. Margaret filled it. Bryce emptied it again. Margaret did not refill it. He looked over his shoulder, but she had already dematerialized on the spot; he could hear her voice in the kitchen, where she was giving instructions to John, who was helping her.

He glanced down at Patty's end of the table, where she seemed to be in ecstasies talking to Nathalie and Ben. She kept clasping her hands with delight and smiling as they detailed their wedding and honeymoon plans. Bryce was disgusted.

He realized he was becoming negligent in his conversational obligation, so he turned to Loretta Jorgensen and asked "So, how are things at the college?" He was instantly sorry he'd chosen that as a starter because she was always too modest to talk about her former work. Meanwhile, she was one of those people who'd had an incredibly fascinating life, and there were any number of other things he could've asked her about and probably learned a great deal. Any story Loretta told was always chock-full of monumental facts and important historical notes. After she had made a few vague remarks about enrollment numbers she'd heard for the upcoming spring semester and it was clear the conversation was going nowhere, he made a better start.

"I understand there was an anthropologist some years ago who was studying a remote tribe in the Pacific, maybe—I don't remember—and he wound up marrying one of the girls in the tribe and bringing her back to America. I always wondered what became of her. Do you know anything about that?" Bryce asked.

"Ah yes, I think I do recall the case you're referencing," Loretta said. Loretta had been raised in some Scandinavian country and she chose her words in English with great care. "I believe the woman returned to her tribe after a while because the dissonance between her experience there and here was too profound to sustain. For example," she continued "Her people knew nothing of technology or any of the modern practices we take for granted. In western society, she became very lonely and withdrawn."

"I think she had a couple of children," Bryce offered.

"Yes, you are right, I think so. They, having had the benefit of an entirely western experience, were able to assimilate into American culture with no difficulty," Loretta said.

"But the tribal woman—she went back?" asked Bryce, pouring himself his second glass of wine.

"Yes. I think maybe when the children were older," Loretta said, finishing a bite of salad. "Of course, by that time, the island had been overrun with anthropologists who'd heard of it by then, so it wasn't the same any more. They had adopted electricity and established a small health center and instituted something of a formal educational system for the children, so—" she paused and shook her head "Not at all the way she had left it."

"What happened to her?" Bryce asked.

"That, I don't know," Loretta said.

"I mean, she obviously didn't fit in in America because of all the technology and everything, but when she went back to the island, everything had changed," Bryce said.

Loretta shrugged. "I suppose she adapted as well as she could; that's what human beings are psychologically and sociologically engineered to do."

"But here she is back on her island," persisted Bryce, "Back on her own island where she grew up, and she understood everything, and she loved her culture, and she never imagined any other existence whatsoever, and then she winds up in this completely different world where she doesn't belong, so she goes back, but it isn't there any more. The old ways are all gone. Partly they're gone because the newcomers destroyed them, and partly they're gone because the islanders started wanting to be part of the outside world instead of being satisfied with what they had. Don't you see?"

"Bryce," said Patty with sudden urgency and a strange look on her face, "Please help me out. What was the name of that film director we were talking about earlier? My memory is atrocious."

Bryce thought a moment. "Slim Whitman," he stated emphatically.

"I think you mean Whit Stillman," said Ben.

"Yes. Of course," Bryce replied. The room was getting hot all of a sudden. He ran his finger under his shirt-collar.

Bryce turned to resume his conversation with Loretta, but she was speaking with her husband Aris, who was seated to her right on the other side.

He turned to his left just as Monsignor Ryan appeared to be turning to address him.

"Well now, did I tell you what happened to me last week?" Monsignor Ryan said.

"No, Monsignor, you didn't," Bryce answered.

"Please—call me Ned," he reminded Bryce, then continued with his story. "Last week Marguerite and I were down in the city because she loves to see all the shop windows decorated for Christmas. Besides, a man can always afford to let his wife window-shop, right? So anyway, we decided we wanted some hot roasted chestnuts, so I told her to wait while I went a little further down the street and got them. Well. When I get back, Ingrid sees I have this perplexed look on my face, so she asks me what's the matter. And I told her 'Twenty years ago, I would've knocked down for saying—in the presence of a young lady—what I just heard a young lady say.' Can you believe it?"

"Yes," agreed Bryce. "It's shocking, the language some of them use." His glass seemed to be empty again and he scanned the table for the wine bottle, which had somehow disappeared. He thought he saw Margaret steal away into the kitchen holding something.

"That's why you're a lucky fellow," Monsignor Ryan said. "This Claudia is a real lady from what I hear. A real lady. You don't find many of those around these days."

Bryce turned to take a sip of wine, remembered his glass was empty, and overheard a snippet of a conversation taking place between Susan, Aris, and Loretta. They were discussing eels.

Eels? thought Bryce. *Who talks about eels?*

He was lost in thought for a moment. Suddenly, he was aware of Monsignor Ryan again, who was saying "Of course, you know what my father would've said."

Bryce realized he must've missed the first half of an ongoing conversation in which he was a participant.

"No," Bryce replied. "What's that?"

"He would've said 'bakers eat their mistakes and doctors bury theirs!'" He laughed.

Bryce laughed too, but he wasn't quite sure why.

He looked down at the end of the table where Patty sat. She was still transfixed by the magic that was Nathalie and Ben. Ben was talking, probably raving about how adorably wonderful Nathalie was, and how lucky he was to have snatched up such an unclaimed treasure.

He tuned back in to Susan's conversation with the Jorgensens.

"It's a significant initiation rite for young men in that country," Loretta was saying.

Aris explained to Susan in an informative tone, "They eat the eel with creamed potatoes and a glass of schnapps."

Meanwhile, directly across the table, Minty's voice was reaching elevated levels. "So she asks 'Where do electrolytes come from, anyway?' and he says 'From electricians!'"

Once the laughter across the table subsided, he could hear Aunt Fluff mid-sentence: "Limitless funds—absolutely *limitless* funds. They're the ones who are ruining the opera. They're the kind that need the English subtitles over the stage. It's appalling. Really, it's appalling."

"Yes," interjected Bryce loudly, to the surprise of Aunt Fluff, himself, and everyone else at the table, who suddenly fell silent.

Leaning forward, he added "But you know what's even more appalling? The fact that we're doomed. Yes, doomed! All of us! We're sitting here having a lovely meal, and meanwhile our entire socioeconomic structure is crumbling because the *nouveau riche* are out-earning us and the Old Guard is intermarrying with the enemy." He shot a look at Ben.

"Bryce!" said Susan.

Ben stared at Bryce in disbelief. Patty looked aghast. Nathalie started to cry.

"Had we defended our civilized ways and not adopted the greedy habits of the social bounders who infiltrated us, we'd still be the masters of our fate. But that's not what hurts the most," Bryce exclaimed. He looked down and realized that his tie was lounging in his salad plate.

"Margaret, get John," instructed Susan sharply, but she had already done so. John entered the dining room and walked around to Bryce's place at the table.

"What hurts the most," Bryce continued dismally, "Is that now we're powerless; scattered to the four winds, and—" he saw John coming up behind him. The next thing he knew, he was on his feet. John and Susan were spiriting him out of the room. He shouted "Don't you understand? John Kenneth Galbraith predicted all of this YEARS ago!"

Bryce was escorted swiftly down the hallway and into the library. The room was cool and dark.

"Thank you, John," he heard Susan saying. She shut the door and John returned to the kitchen.

Bryce felt a warm blanket being thrown over him. He realized he was sitting in a wingchair with his feet on an ottoman.

"Margaret is bringing some coffee," Susan said.

Bryce looked up at her. He felt bad. He knew he had disrupted the party.

"Am I a bad brother?" he asked.

"No," Susan replied. "You're just stinking drunk."

Bryce started to stand up. "I've got to apologize," he said.

"Not now," Susan said, pushing him firmly back into the chair. "I think everyone's heard enough out of you for one night. Just rest."

Bryce vaguely perceived a shadow in the doorway and then there was a tray next to him with coffee, toast, and a glass of water.

Susan sat with him as he ate and drank. In the softly lit room, she was pretty. He could tell she wasn't angry. She was always good in a crisis. His very own Jeanne d'Arc.

He became sleepy and Susan held his hand for a little while. Then he napped.

When he woke up, Patty and John were there.

"Hey," said Patty, smiling. He smiled back until he remembered what he had done.

"Oh my God," he said, scrambling to get up.

"Easy there," said Patty. "We're taking you upstairs."

She and John helped him to his feet. He felt very woozy once he was standing.

They brought him out of the library and started up the stairs. From the dining room, he could hear Susan saying "Mother always said the best exercise was shaking your head 'no' to seconds."

Everyone laughed.

19

In the morning, Bryce would've been frantic if he were feeling up to it. He tried to catalogue his sins of the previous night: he had insulted Ben, insinuated that Nathalie's engagement was responsible for the downfall of polite society, and been loud and drunk, ruining Susan and Patty's Christmas dinner and embarrassing all their guests. Then there was John . . . something about John; finally, he remembered that John had helped him upstairs and into bed.

He didn't know how he was ever going to face the Mastersons again. He realized this was probably the worst thing he had ever done.

He heard a light knock at the door and Susan poked her head in.

"How are we doing this morning?" she asked.

"Oh God, Susan—I'm sorry—I'm so, so sorry," Bryce said.

Susan came in. She had a tray with coffee, orange juice, and toast.

"Don't get up. Margaret prepared this for you. It'll help," Susan said, putting the tray in front of him.

Bryce downed the juice immediately and took a deep breath.

"I don't know what came over me," Bryce said.

Susan sat down in the chair next to the bed. "I think it was a lot of things," she said. "Your inheritance, jitters about your engagement, the first Christmas without Grandfather," she explained.

Bryce wasn't entirely sure about the last item, but he said "Still, that was no excuse for ruining a dinner party and embarrassing myself in front of all your guests. I can't even imagine what Ben must think," Bryce said, shaking his head.

"He was very understanding," Susan said, adding "They have drunks in China, too." She smiled at him. That made him feel a little better.

"But Bryce, seriously—invoking the name of John Kenneth Galbraith? What did you even mean by that?" she asked.

"I don't know," Bryce responded. "It sounded good at the time."

"Patty and I were up half the night trying to figure that one out," she said.

Bryce was stung afresh with guilt at the mention of Patty's name. "Is she very upset?" he asked.

"She was pretty mortified, for the guests' sake, but she'll forgive you," Susan said. "She doesn't like to think of anyone hurting someone else in our home."

Bryce put his head in his hands.

"Bryce," Susan said reassuringly, "Patty loves you. She'll get over it."

"How am I ever going to apologize to everyone?" he asked.

"You know what Mother would say if she were here," Susan said. "Start writing those letters."

20

After resting a bit and taking a shower, Bryce was packed and ready to go in a few hours. Margaret sent John up to get his things.

"John," Bryce said as the boy was about to pick up his bags, "I'm really sorry about last night."

John shook his head. "Listen, don't worry about it." He turned to go.

"No, really," Bryce said, waylaying him. "I apologize for putting you in an awkward position. That wasn't fair of me, and I want you to know I appreciate your kindness. Wrangling drunks shouldn't be part of your job description."

"Like I said, it's okay," John said, making his way down the hallway.

Bryce went downstairs a moment later and apologized profusely to Patty. She was very sweet about it but he could tell she was uneasy. He had outraged her hospitality. It would take time to earn back her trust. He knew Susan would advocate for him, but he realized it would probably be a while before he was able to visit the house again. That would be his punishment.

That, and having to face Nathalie and Ben, which was, Bryce realized, only a matter of seconds away, as he saw the two of them actually walking towards the house.

"Bryce," Nathalie said as they approached. "We were coming to see how you were today. I made some cookies for you." She handed Bryce a wrapped plate piled high with his favorite sugar cookies.

"Nathalie, Ben," he said looking at them both, "I don't even know where to begin—"

Ben interrupted him. "Please; no harm done, no hard feelings." He extended his hand.

Bryce shook Ben's hand. "I can only say that I hope I'll prove myself worthy of your forgiveness. I didn't mean what I said last night, honestly. I'm very happy for you and Nathalie and I wish you both nothing but the very best."

"Thank you," said Ben. "If there's ever anything we can do for you, let us know."

"Susan said you're going through a bit of a rough time," Nathalie said with a note of pity in her voice. She smiled a sad smile. "I understand," she said. She was so sweet. He felt like an absolute heel to have made her cry.

Bryce was suddenly anxious to get away, so after exchanging a few pleasantries about the upcoming new year, he said goodbye and drove home.

Back in Larchmont, he unpacked his things. Somehow, Margaret had gotten the salad dressing stains out of his tie. He was glad because it was one of his favorites, a Turnbull & Asser that had belonged to his father.

He pulled out his writing paper and dashed off the letters to Uncle Clement and Aunt Fluff, the Mastersons, the Jorgensens, and the Ryans. He would post them immediately. He'd composed the text that morning at Susan's, where the weight of shame was still tangible.

Putting the cap on his pen and sitting back in his chair, he reflected on the incident from a sober perspective. He wasn't given to excessive drinking, and contrary to Susan's analysis, he didn't think it was because of the recent events in his life.

He looked out the window at the snow on Boston Post Road. A memory came to mind of a winter's day when he was a teen. It was about this time of year; his school had dismissed at noon, but he had told his mother he would be staying there afterwards. He didn't recall why, perhaps to meet a friend. At any rate, some local hoodlums about his own age approached him as he sat on one of the stone benches out front. At first, he thought they would just pass by, but they stopped and asked him the time. Something about them worried him, but he reminded himself that just because they weren't fellow classmates of his at the exclusive prep school didn't mean they couldn't relate to each other. Perhaps they were just guys who felt the need to look tough but were actually just like him underneath. As he was looking down at his watch, about to report the time, he felt hands on his ankles and from behind, an arm was wrapped around his throat. They lifted him up and as they choked him, they pulled him towards the school building.

"Stop!" he managed to shout.

He remembered being called names. He struggled to free himself but it was no use, there were too many of them. He tried to figure out what they were planning to do to him. Maybe they were going to throw him into one of the deep piles of snow alongside the breezeway, which they were fast approaching. Whatever their intention, it was no longer a joke. Bryce didn't like it and he wasn't going to have it. The kidding had gone far enough.

"Put me down, now!" he commanded.

At this, they merely laughed, which outraged him. He'd tried to be a good sport, but now there would be serious consequences; he would call the authorities down on them.

"Put me down or I'll scream for help," he warned angrily. He hoped that between them they had lengthy enough criminal records that the prospect of adding more offenses would be a deterrent.

"You can yell your head off for all we care," one of them said. "There's nobody here."

In a chilling instant, Bryce realized that what he said was true. The school was closed. The nearest house was well out of earshot. The parking lot, which would normally be full of cars, was completely empty. There wasn't a soul in the building; even the janitors were gone.

After gasping for breath, he took stock of the situation. They were dragging him into one of the concrete stairwells to the basement. He had about fifty dollars in his wallet. He hoped they wouldn't take his watch or break any bones.

After throwing him down in a corner against the basement door, they kicked him in the jaw. Several more kicks landed in his stomach. Involuntarily, he lurched forward at that point, feeling that he was about to heave his guts up, when another kick connected with his eye and sent his head flying backwards. It hit the concrete wall. The pain melted into disorientation. They were pulling him; pawing at him. His coat was being jostled around. Someone spit on him, then another. He heard them laugh as they walked away.

He managed to get up and make his way back to the school's entrance by the road. He was clutching his stomach and his blood was leaving a trail of little scarlet droplets in the snow as he went. He wasn't sure exactly where he would go, but before he could decide, the mother of one of his classmates who lived nearby who was passing the school stopped her car when she saw him and brought him home.

All in all, the doctor said he'd be fine. He had a concussion and a black eye, but no broken ribs. They'd taken his wallet, but not his watch. They probably didn't have any idea what a Patek Philippe was worth, he thought with a chagrin. Their lack of sophistication was one of the small blessings he could count from the incident.

At the police station later, he gave a report but he knew it wasn't much to go on. Driving home, his father told him he'd done well, and said that he might still feel fearful for a while afterwards; that was normal after being assaulted. But Bryce wasn't thinking of that at all. What terrified him the most was recollecting that moment when he knew that he could scream and scream and nobody would hear him.

21

Bryce woke up from his nap and stared at the ceiling. This was the most delicious time of year, the lazy week between Christmas and New Year's Day. Unfortunately, it was being ruined by his indecision about what to do about Claudia.

He had reservations at the restaurant where they'd had their first date. He would order champagne and propose after it arrived. The chef was making a special cake for their dessert.

Everyone approved. Everyone was behind him. He didn't doubt that Claudia would say yes.

It was just the part after that which he couldn't get a handle on. Not where they'd live or what they'd do, but what they were to each other.

Each objection that came to mind was countered by some bit of golden advice. If he found her uninteresting, it wasn't a valid criticism because she was a wife, not an entertainer. If he found her dull, it meant he needed to focus on making his own life more remarkable. The predictable habits into which they were already quickly slipping were to be desired, not disdained, and whatever uncharted life he felt he was relinquishing by marrying her was to be filed squarely under the heading of "Greener Grass."

Marrying Claudia would be an act of maturity, wisdom, and self-fulfillment. She would bring good things into his life; they would be happy. Eventually, they would not be able to imagine existence without each other.

Bryce supposed it was the same with parenthood. The initial fearful, overwhelmed feeling would be replaced in time by joy and enhanced well-being.

But maybe there was something wrong with him. He wasn't above considering that possibility. Maybe he was one of those flaky old bachelors who'd never get married. Or he'd wait until he was sixty and marry some twenty-year-old and start have children.

There was one thing that Bryce knew: in the sea of rising and falling emotions, the one thing that could be counted upon was a certain way of doing things. That Aunt Bitsy, Sarah, Patty, and everyone else in their circle agreed unanimously that this was a good move caused Bryce to lend it more weight in his ruminations than the wildly swinging pendulum of feelings he was experiencing. Put simply, marrying Claudia was the right thing to do. He resigned himself to it.

He thought about calling Claudia and seeing if she wanted to wander around the mall. He hated the mall like poison, but this time of year, it was fun to go there for a while and pretend to be an ordinary person. She would probably not want to go. Maybe he could find a holiday concert or something at a local church that they could attend.

Then he remembered that she was in Oyster Bay with her brother and his family. On Christmas Eve, she called him before they left for the Lessons & Carols service. Her brother attended the same church where Theodore Roosevelt worshipped. Claudia said that it was lovely at Christmastime.

Bryce felt like calling Deek, but that woman would probably be with him, swearing like a sailor in the background. He thought about seeing if Rohan felt like doing anything, since as far as he knew, the frog-killing fiancée had not yet set one murderous foot on American soil, but he thought the idea of two reluctant prospective grooms getting together was a recipe for disaster.

Then he thought of Cristina. He owed her a call.

When she picked up, she sounded delighted to hear from him, as always.

"How are you?" she asked.

He explained that he was well and that he'd spent Christmas with Susan and Patty. He omitted the drunken incident. He asked about her.

"Things are just fabulous," she said. Things were always fabulous with her. "My stepdaughter's wedding is in February, and everyone is quite excited, let me tell you."

"He's a French nobleman, right? Where's the wedding?" asked Bryce.

"Monaco," she replied. "It's a long story, but he has ties there. And we're getting The Gypsy Queens for the reception," she said.

"That's great," Bryce said.

"Well, that's what Catalina wanted," she explained, "But personally, I'm sick of them. They're at every party you go to, you know? After a while it's like, you want something else."

"I understand," Bryce agreed.

"Hey, you know what?" Cristina asked. "I'm going to be a little-old-lady mother of the bride!"

Bryce recalled that Catalina's mother was dead—Cristina's husband was a widower—so Cristina would be fulfilling the official mother-role.

"You, a little old lady? I don't think so," Bryce shot back. Cristina laughed.

"Seriously," she said, still giggling, "I have this very pale peach dress with beads on it—I mean, I look like 'The Golden Girls' or whatever that show was."

Bryce almost guffawed out loud. "I highly doubt that," he said. "You always look spectacular. You could still pass for twenty—easily."

"Well, I had a little work done last year; nothing radical, but I look well-rested all the time," she said. "You should see some of them, though. It's nothing like those Hollywood people over there, but we have our share over here with those over-pulled, frozen faces. Ugh!"

"What else is going on over there?" Bryce asked. He was glad Cristina was a bit self-obsessed because it saved him from having to talk about himself.

"The usual. It's very difficult and it's only getting worse," she admitted. "One of my friends in England is turning her castle into a timeshare, and another one is doing the guest-house thing.

Nobody can afford to heat those old monsters anymore. It's crazy. I couldn't bear strangers in my house. I don't know how they do it."

"Sounds like it's not a matter of choice; it's that or lose the farm," Bryce said. "You're not in any danger, are you?" he asked.

"Oh no, we're very solid, but so many of my friends aren't. Even the ones with the big names. It's almost unimaginable that their houses would fall. Of course, some of them are really making the best of it. There's a count in Milan who became like this hippie guy; he grows vegetables for community sustainability and sells them to the locals. I think he has a pigtail and everything. He's rebranding his nobility as the reason that he has to care for the townspeople, like some benevolent king in a fairy tale. I think he's also trying to undo all the evil karma from his grandfather, who used to beat the men and force himself on the servant girls. Everybody knew about it, but a lot of them were like that in those times."

"Ah, the good old days," said Bryce sarcastically.

"You're terrible!" Cristina said, laughing.

Bryce said "A lot of the old families are doing the same thing here, downplaying their wealth and pretending they identify with the masses."

"It's so crazy, isn't it? They're trying to act like they don't have money so the hordes won't behead them when the revolution comes," Cristina said.

"Nah, there isn't going to be any revolution," Bryce predicted. "They'll never get their act together." At this, Cristina laughed even harder.

"What about you?" she asked. "What's going on with your small fortune?"

Bryce told her a bit about the cabin in Norfolk.

"It sounds charming! I'd love to see it someday," she said.

Finally, Bryce knew he could put off the inevitable no longer.

"I'm thinking of getting married," he said.

"Bryce! That's magnificent!" she exclaimed. "Who is it?"

Bryce told Cristina all about Claudia. Cristina said she was vaguely familiar with the name and knew something about Claudia's father's manufacturing plants in Europe.

"Well done, sweetheart," Cristina said. "That's one decision you'll never regret."

Bryce suddenly blurted out "I think I regret it already."

"What?" said Cristina. Her voice was a mix of genuine surprise and concern. "What are you talking about? What are you regretting?"

Bryce broke down and told her about his confusion, his indecision, and a lot of other extraneous things that probably didn't make any sense, but had been swirling around in his mind lately.

He heard Cristina exhale sharply, and then waited for her to speak.

"Dear, dear Bryce," she said calmly. "Listen to me. All these ideas you have—you're not sure you'll be happy with her, she's so dull, whatever—these are little-boy worries." She paused a moment. "Can I tell you something in a friendly way? About us?"

"Sure," said Bryce, but he thought that with an ominous lead-in like that, maybe he'd wind up wishing he'd said no.

"When we were going out together, I really liked you. You're very charming and you're very funny in your own way."

In my own way? thought Bryce. *What the hell does she mean by that?*

"However," she continued "I knew that marrying you would be like gambling. And you know I don't gamble, right? With you, I didn't know are we going to have money, are we going to raise our children well—there was too much uncertainty for the future, and I didn't want that."

"But can anyone really have—" Bryce interrupted.

"Ah, ah, ah—just a moment, please—let me finish," Cristina chided. "So there I was and I'm wondering why you were like that, and my father explained to me that when a man is immature, he throws his future into the wind like a handful of seeds."

Oh great, now she's telling me the story of Jack and the Beanstalk, Bryce thought, angrily.

"But when a man is sure of himself," she continued "He plans his life with care and plants and waters those seeds so he can have a good harvest. Do you understand?"

"So, are you the seeds or the water? Or perhaps one of the lovely melons?" Bryce asked.

"Now you're upset with me?" Cristina asked. He could tell from her tone of voice that she was scowling.

Bryce realized he wasn't, but he was sick of being lectured about maturity. Cristina hadn't had to drop out of college because she was broke. She hadn't subsisted for years on ridiculously low salaries. She'd never seen a utility shut-off notice.

"Cristina, I'm not upset. I'm hearing what you have to say; really. I'm listening. And I genuinely respect your opinion," Bryce explained. "But your point is that because I broke away from my family, I was immature, and that's simply not true."

"Bryce," Cristina explained in a serious tone, "To turn your back on your family—not just the people—but the heritage and the role that you were expected to play, is—" she sought for a word that she couldn't find. She continued. "Then there is the matter of those advantages, and what you could have done with them. Can you honestly say that you've done better on your own than you could've with their money and connections?"

"Of course not," said Bryce. "I'd probably be the CEO of some massive corporation or head of a foundation right now. I know that."

"Right," Christina said. "So that's two strikes against you. And finally, if you'd wanted me to share that life with you, that would've shown that you had no regard for me. The money wasn't an issue—I had more than enough—but to drag me along on your goose-chase and ruin our own future; I couldn't have that. So I'm coming up with 'immature' because you were a man who didn't take up his responsibilities, threw away every advantage, and expected me to make all the sacrifices."

"Well," conceded Bryce, "But only from a certain point of view."

"What point of view?" She asked. "There's only one point of view. And now, you're back with your family, you have your inheritance, and you're marrying a woman whom you can share a good life with. You can have your social circles, you can have children—and together you are building something, not lost in a wilderness."

"So you're saying I'm nervous because I'm being mature for the first time in my life?" Bryce summarized.

"Simply put, yes. That's it," Cristina said. "And I hope you're not having bad feelings towards me now for telling you the truth as your friend."

Cristina's friendship was not something Bryce doubted. It was her insight that upset him. Clearly, she lived by her own advice and had a stable marriage with a powerful and wealthy man whom she saw about thirty days a year.

Bryce also realized that what Cristina had said was exactly what everyone else who knew and cared about him had said, in not so many words. In fact, Rohan was basically going through an identical scenario, albeit with a slight variation, and Bryce himself had tried to convince him to marry the woman.

He paused a moment, and then asked Cristina "Are you happy?"

Without hesitation, she replied. "Yes. I have everything I need; I have a good life. I'm very fulfilled by my role in my marriage and in my family and in my friendships. I'm at liberty to do whatever I want. Even a queen doesn't have that."

Bryce paused again. There was nothing insincere about her response.

"Maybe I just want more than you do," he concluded.

"More?" she asked. "What more? I have everything in the world and I know it."

She sighed again. "Bryce, I'm not going to tell you what to do—you have to live your own life—but if you are asking me, I think you will be happier and better off if you marry Claudia."

"You do?" asked Bryce.

"Yes, I do. I believe it very strongly," she added.

Suddenly he had déjà vu and he was back in the conversation with Aunt Bitsy in which she suggested marrying Claudia.

He thanked Cristina and told her that he did appreciate her counsel more than he could possibly express. He told her he would go through with the engagement. They said their goodbyes and Cristina promised to send him photos from Catalina's wedding.

"Bryce," Cristina said right before they hung up.

"Yes?" he said.

"I'm very proud of you," she said.

22

"I am fully willing to own up to the fact that I'm one of those awful people who always needs to do something splashy on New Year's Eve," Bryce told Claudia when they arrived at the restaurant. She smiled.

"I mean, I couldn't possibly imagine being someone who just says 'Happy New Year' aloud while watching the ball drop on TV, or worse, one of those people who actually falls asleep way before midnight, as if it were just any night," he explained.

He ordered champagne, noticing that his hand was trembling a little as he held the wine list.

Even though it probably only took a few minutes for the bottle to arrive, it seemed like an eternity to Bryce. Claudia wasn't particularly talkative but she looked very nice. She was wearing a pearl grey dress and had her hair up. He complimented her appearance. She thanked him.

When the waiter came and opened the bottle, Bryce thought he flashed him a conspicuously big smile.

How could he possibly know? he wondered, then remembered. *Oh, the cake—that's right, the cake.* Probably the whole kitchen staff was aglow with romantic joy at the thought of the engagement.

Before they took their first sip of champagne, Bryce explained to Claudia that he had something to ask her, presented the ring, and asked her to marry him. He didn't remember exactly what he had said. He'd rehearsed something beforehand, but in the moment, he strayed a bit from the script, although evidently, he got the point across because she said yes. She appeared very pleased with the ring. Aunt Bitsy had steered him right.

During dinner, they discussed the future. Apparently, Claudia had already decided where they should go on their honeymoon and she had an a few towns in mind for when they returned where she had done some preliminary investigation about house-prices. It dawned on Bryce with no small disappointment that the proposal hadn't been a complete surprise to Claudia and he wondered if Aunt Bitsy had spilled the beans or if Claudia was just a particularly perceptive woman.

She explained that she'd like to continue working until they started a family, at which point she would switch over to the charity circuit. She had several favorite non-profits from which she said she'd like to choose.

Now that they were engaged, Bryce wanted to ask her exactly what horribly perverted thing her ex-fiancé had done to cause their breakup, but he didn't feel it would be appropriate. Still, he burned with curiosity. So far, on the few occasions they had been intimate, she hadn't seemed shocked by anything, so he didn't think she had spurned the ex out of any bizarre prudishness. Still, he wondered.

After dinner, they returned to Bryce's apartment and rang in the new year together. Normally, he would've gotten tickets to a ball or accepted an invitation to a party, but he thought she might prefer to spend the time together quietly on this particular night. She called her mother and brother. Bryce called Susan and Aunt Bitsy. Everyone sounded elated and somewhat relieved.

The next day, they went for an extravagant brunch. When they returned to his apartment, there were a flood of messages from well-wishers. The phone continued to ring throughout the day.

Late in the afternoon, as Claudia and Bryce watched an old movie and considered what to have for dinner, the phone rang again. Bryce answered.

"This is Ashley," said an unfamiliar woman's voice.

"Just a moment," said Bryce, turning to Claudia. He whispered "I think it's for you."

"I haven't given anyone your number," she whispered back.

Puzzled, he returned to the call. "Hi Ashley, I think you have the wrong number."

"Is this Bryce?" she asked.

"Yes, it is," he responded.

"I'm Leslie's sister," she explained.

"Oh," said Bryce, completely confused. "How is she?"

"She's dead," Ashley said.

"Dead?" Bryce asked. "What happened?"

"She killed herself last night. She swallowed a couple bottles of pills," Ashley explained. "Your name was in her contacts list, so I thought you should know."

Suicide. I should've seen that coming, Bryce thought. He knew she was unstable but he hadn't realized how bad off she truly was.

Ashley continued matter-of-factly. "I guess she was lonely, it was New Year's Eve—whatever—she was dead by the time they found her," she said.

"I'm . . . terribly sorry, Ashley," he said. "I was a friend of hers," he explained. "Is there anything I can do? Anything you need?"

"No, we've got it all covered here. My brother Dylan came from Pittsburgh and a lot of my neighbors are helping us out," she said.

"Are you sure there's nothing?" Bryce asked.

"No, really, we're good," she said. "I just thought you should know, that's all. I wouldn't want you calling her and getting a bad surprise." Her voice broke a little and it sounded like she was going to cry.

"Thank you," Bryce said. "That was very considerate of you."

"Well, I've got a few others to call, so I have to go," Ashley said, making a sniffling sound.

"Just a minute—what about a viewing? Has anything been planned yet?" he asked.

"You mean like a funeral? No, we've decided to scatter her ashes at the beach," she said.

"Well . . . are there any charities to which contributions should be sent?" he asked.

"I guess you could send them anywhere," she answered vaguely. "She liked animals."

"I see," he said. "Well, thank you again and I'm terribly sorry for your loss."

"Thanks," she said and hung up.

Bryce had a vague recollection of Leslie mentioning a married sister and some other family members who lived in Pittsburgh.

Ashley had mentioned calling other friends. He wondered if Graham was on that list. He wondered if Ashley knew the nature of the relationship between Leslie and Graham.

"Who was that?" Claudia asked.

Bryce sat down beside her. She'd turned the TV off as soon as she heard him say "dead."

"That was the sister of a friend of mine. Her name was Leslie. Apparently, she committed suicide last night," he explained.

"Oh, how awful. I'm so sorry," she said.

"Yes, the sister said she was lonely and swallowed a couple of bottles of pills," Bryce said.

"Does she have children?" Claudia asked.

"Just a sister and a brother, from what it sounds like. I didn't know her extremely well, we met a few years ago and she would mostly come over to talk about boyfriend problems," he explained.

"Poor thing," Claudia said. "When is the funeral?"

Bryce shrugged. “They’re just having her cremated and scattering her ashes. They’re not doing a wake or anything. She made it sound like nobody was invited to the ash-scattering.”

“What a shame,” Claudia said. “Do you think it’s because—” she trailed off.

“No, I think it’s just because they’re very informal. Leslie was a pretty casual person,” he explained.

“Oh,” said Claudia. She gave him a hug.

“I asked if there were anything I could do, but she said no,” Bryce said.

“Then I guess that’s it,” Claudia said.

“Yes, I guess so,” Bryce agreed.

Claudia had an early meeting the next day, so they decided to postpone dinner. She went home.

After she left, Bryce thought again of Leslie. He imagined her in some horribly deluded state, probably thinking that life wasn’t worth living if she couldn’t have Graham. It sickened him to think that.

He knew he should call Deek and Rohan and tell them about the engagement but he didn’t feel like it. He ordered some sushi and went down to pick it up. The fresh night air was bracing and felt good. In the quiet darkness with nothing but snow around, his thoughts seemed magnified.

He didn’t quite know what to make of Leslie’s death. Maybe she was better off. Should he feel guilty that they weren’t on speaking terms at the time of her suicide? If they had been, would it have made a difference?

Judging from the fact that nothing he ever did for her seemed to help, he surmised that having been in touch with him on or before New Year’s Eve wouldn’t have changed matters a bit. If anything, he probably would’ve told her to forget about Graham, she would’ve swallowed the pills, and the outcome would’ve been the same.

And what about Graham? This would be a bonus for him: no loose ends. No crazy ex to inform his wife about the affair or ruin his future plans with Romy and whomever else he had lined up.

For a fleeting second, he wondered if Graham could’ve actually murdered Leslie and made it look like a suicide. While it was possible, he doubted Graham would go that far. If he were that worried about his wife (or anyone else, for that matter) finding out about his infidelities, he would’ve been a lot more discreet in public and in the office.

No, this was just a plain old suicide. Leslie’s life hadn’t amounted to very much, and she’d made some terrible choices, right down to her very last one.

Bryce sighed. He was sorry she’d come to such a dismal end.

After dinner, he took a hot shower and went to bed.

23

In his dreams, Bryce found himself on a lone country road. The sky was grey and he felt a sense of desolation. He heard something.

Turning to look, he saw a small group of people in the distance, dressed in black, walking in single-file. The leader carried a box. They were indistinct, but they were moving with intention, as though they were one being. He watched as they left the road and walked into the forest, uncertain where they were headed.

He left the road himself to see where they were going, and followed them, staying out of sight. Eventually, after winding his way through twigs and stepping on dead branches that crunched underfoot, he saw the river.

The people stood on the bank and opened the box and a swirl of ashes hovered in the air briefly before settling onto the waters and being carried away by the current. He realized the ashes were Leslie's. The box closed and the group turned and went back the way they came, as silently and intentionally as before.

There was something peaceful in the event he had just witnessed, but at the same time, he felt something was wrong; disastrously wrong. Little pieces of Leslie were in disarray and being carried apart by the water. Some may have clung to the air or floated to the ground. She was being scattered in all directions—disassembled--destroyed.

He began breathing hard, realizing the implications and trying desperately to think of how to collect her and put her back together when a violent cry nearby startled him. Something was crashing through the underbrush and moving quickly towards him. He ran immediately towards the river, having nowhere else to go.

The pursuit continued, and his heart pounded madly as he fled, too terrified to look behind him. He watched his footing lest he stumble, because he knew the things that were after him were close behind. His only hope was to outrun them. There was a lot of distance to cover, and he ran with all his might.

When he got to the river he plunged forward without hesitation, hoping that somehow, on the other side, he would be safe. He took no notice of anything; the only thought that guided him was making his way to the opposite shore. Gradually, the sounds behind him died away.

PART TWO

24

Being engaged, it seemed to Bryce, had set into motion a million things that had been waiting for him to ask that one little question. A party to celebrate the announcement was quickly followed by decisions about venue and other details. He tried to stay out of everyone's way as much as possible, and everyone seemed perfectly fine with that arrangement. He was only called upon when absolutely necessary.

Deek and Rohan had, of course, offered their heartiest congratulations upon hearing the news, but he could tell that neither of them was being honest. More accurately, they were genuinely happy for his good fortune and certainly wished him luck, but there was some sense of silent acknowledgement that it was a thing to be done; to be made the best of. It gave rise to perplexing feelings.

On the other hand, Bryce was being universally showered with approval. All the women of his acquaintance smiled when they saw him now. Married men started treating him like an equal and taking his opinions more seriously than he thought they ever had before. He'd crossed an invisible threshold. He was in the club.

Claudia was affectionate and loyal. She would cuddle up next to him as they sat on the couch together in his apartment. She appeared to be contented. She planned their wedding and honeymoon shrewdly, and he was thankful that she didn't seem to be the kind of woman who wanted to throw a lot money around. Everything she did was in quiet good taste. He was proud of her. She made him look good.

One evening he'd been telling her a story about the days when he was teaching and how he had to take the bus to school because he couldn't afford a necessary repair on his car when she wrinkled her nose a little.

“Can we maybe not talk about that?” she asked.

“About what, the car?” he asked.

She looked away. “About those days,” she said. “Let's look forward. I think that's better.”

Bryce remembered that this wasn't the first time she'd shrunk from discussing his past. It seemed everything up until the time he left the family was fine, and everything since Grandfather's death was fine, but anything in between wasn't a fitting subject and was a part of his life she'd rather he allowed everyone to forget.

He wasn't sure what to say in response, so he changed the subject.

“Did I tell you about the film I saw last night?” he asked.

“No,” she said, brightening to the new topic.

"Mind you, I was bored," he explained, "And I was flipping channels and came across it and since it was just starting, I thought I might as well watch it. It starred that dopey blonde—you know, the one who thinks she can act."

Claudia offered a few actresses' names, but Bryce said she was wrong.

He clarified, "The one who used to be married to that guy—the one everyone says is secretly gay."

Claudia said she didn't know who he meant and encouraged him to continue his story.

"Anyway," he said, "she was playing some kind of unstable character, which she did remarkably well, but she was supposed to be from New England and she did a horrible job with the dialect. The story was about this woman whose rich husband dies under mysterious circumstances and she's raising her daughter alone in this creepy house."

"Was it a horror film?" asked Claudia.

"Well, that's the thing," explained Bryce. "It starts out like a serious film but then little by little, all these bizarre things keep happening, and you don't know if it's someone trying to make her believe she's crazy so they can get her money, or if she's really losing her mind, or what. So I sit through two hours of this," he continued. "She starts acting more and more unhinged and more and more unexplained things keep happening, and then guess what happens?"

"What?" asked Claudia.

"It's over. That's it. You're supposed to decide for yourself if it was evil spirits or whatever. Can you believe it?" he said.

"Well, yes," Claudia replied.

"Yes? Maybe this is some kind of very hip, modern style of filmmaking, but you can keep it as far as I'm concerned," Bryce said.

"Really?" Claudia said.

"And that's not all," he added. "Would you believe the glowing reviews this thing received? I looked it up. It won a slew of awards. Unbelievable," he concluded.

"Bryce, maybe you don't understand the symbolism, or you're not being objective enough about the director's vision," Claudia suggested gently.

"The director's vision?" Bryce repeated sarcastically. "I think the director went to get coffee ten minutes into the film and never came back."

Claudia said, "I haven't seen the film so I can't offer an informed opinion, but I bet there's more to this that you just didn't understand."

Bryce bristled. "Why would you assume that?" he asked.

Claudia hesitated a moment. "You don't seem particularly informed when it comes to modern art," she said plainly.

Bryce was suddenly angry. "Oh, you mean like that garbage that you throw grants at all day? The Great Tin Foil Retrospective? Sand art?"

"Bryce, that's not fair," Claudia said.

"No—you're right," Bryce said. "I'm too lowbrow to appreciate this cinematographic masterpiece. Just like how I can't understand those artsy films you love that you can't even explain to me unless you read the review first in *The New Yorker*."

Claudia put her coat on and picked up her handbag. "I'm sorry you're not in a good mood. I'll be going now," she said as she left.

Bryce knew he should probably stop her, but he didn't want to. All at once, he was feeling suffocated. She was wearing his diamond. She'd come back. He hoped she'd take her time.

A few minutes later, the phone rang. He hurried to pick it up, thinking it was Claudia calling to apologize, but it was Deek.

"Hi Bryce," said Deek. "Tiffany and I are in the neighborhood and we just wondered if you and Claudia would like to join us for Mexican."

Even though he disliked last-minute invitations, on this occasion, Bryce welcomed the idea. The fight with Claudia had made him hungry.

"I'm on my own," he explained. "I can meet you there in ten minutes."

"Don't bother," said Deek, "We're on our way upstairs." He hung up.

Bryce let them in while he went into the bedroom to put on a fresh shirt. He had a feeling Tiffany was light-fingered and he hoped Deek was keeping an eye on her.

The restaurant was just down the street. The brightly colored interior decoration and festive Mexican music put Bryce in a cheerful mood.

Tiffany gave her order to their waiter first. Somehow, she managed to say "quesadilla" in such a way that it rhymed with "armadillo." Once, in an Italian restaurant, Bryce had heard one of Deek's dates pronounce "prosciutto" so that it rhymed with "mosquito." *Where does he find these women?* he wondered.

Deek looked upbeat, but tense. He always looked like that around his girlfriends.

"So," Tiffany said, sipping her Margarita, "We invited to the wedding?"

Ignoring the gaffe, Bryce simply replied "Of course."

"Good," she said. "I can't wait to try some of that top-shelf liquor I know you'll be serving."

"Actually," Bryce said, "It's going to be a very modest affair. Claudia has simple tastes."

"Yeah," said Tiffany. "I bet." She smirked. "You gonna have that kind that has bits of real gold floating in the bottle?"

What does she think we are, drug dealers? Bryce wondered. He chose to find her remark amusing and forced himself to laugh lightly. "No, we won't be having that," he explained.

"It must be nice to have whatever you want," she remarked.

Deek intervened to quell an awkward situation before it got out of hand. "Honey, Bryce and Claudia are just regular folks. I've told you that."

Tiffany gave him a look of disbelief. "Oh yeah, you mean 'regular' like your family, who owns an island," she stated ungrammatically.

"It's a very small island," Deek clarified.

"Have you met Deek's family?" Bryce asked. If things were going to get edgy, he might as well dive right in.

"She met my mom briefly during the holidays," Deek reported.

Tiffany laughed. "So get this—Deek brings me over their house and I thought the guy who answered the door was his father. Turns out it's the butler or whoever. So Lurch brings us into their giant living room and there's Deek's mom and his sisters and they're like totally horrified to see me, but they're doing this rich-person pretend thing where they're being all polite. It was a riot."

"My mom and my sisters just weren't expecting anyone as pretty as you," Deek said.

Tiffany laughed harder. "Yeah, right!" she snorted. Bryce looked around to see if any other diners had noticed.

Bryce wanted to change the subject. He was going to ask Tiffany about her travels, or where she'd gone to school, or what occupied her days, but he felt each line of inquiry was worse than the next. She had long nails with designs painted on them. Maybe he could ask about that.

"Your nails are very artistic. Do you paint them yourself?" It was a sorry subject, but it was the best he could do. He was hoping their meal would be served soon.

"Nah," said Tiffany, "I have them done at this Korean place. They even give you this kung-fu chop massage while you're waiting for them to dry. It's cool." Bryce had absolutely no idea what she was talking about. He looked at Deek. Long years of companionship allowed him to deduce that Deek had no idea what she was talking about, either.

He tried to look at Tiffany as objectively as possible. He had to admit that there was something attractive about her. She was chubby with thick, dark red hair, but she had lovely green eyes and long eyelashes. She carried herself well and had good posture. She had an air of confidence which Bryce had definitely never seen in any of Deek's previous girlfriends.

Their dinner arrived and Bryce watched as she daintily picked up her quesadilla and ate it at such a leisurely pace that there was something almost regal about how she did it. He tried not to stare at her napkin, which remained beside her plate throughout the meal.

Deek did most of the talking, but when Tiffany did speak, she made some clever insights. Bryce figured she had half a brain and perhaps if she'd had a decent education, she might have amounted to something. He also discovered that she was easy to talk to. As much as he hated to admit it, it was refreshing to converse with someone who appeared to say whatever popped into their head.

What fascinated him about her most, though, was that she had this "I've got your number" sort of expression with which she looked at him. Bryce could've written it off as her thinking she understood him because to her, all rich people lived in a huge bottle filled with trendy liquor and floating shards of gold, but he sensed she was more intuitive than that.

Tiffany's phone rang. Deek put his hand on hers and plaintively said "Not now, Hon," but she shoved his hand off, picked it up, and answered.

Deek and Bryce looked at each other between bites of their dinner, pretending not to be hearing her side of a conversation with someone named Izzy that involved a fight with a boyfriend who was committing acts of infidelity with his co-worker at a fast-food restaurant on the counter after hours.

When the call was over, Tiffany shared tidbits of the conversation to fill out the picture for the men.

"He's banging this drug-bag he works with," she explained. "I told Izzy she needs to dump his ass. Besides, he's a creep. He likes to watch her doing it with other guys."

Neither Bryce nor Deek knew the appropriate response to that, so they both simply said "Oh," almost in unison. Their childhood etiquette training hadn't let them down.

25

Bryce reconciled with Claudia the next day. He'd sat around all morning reading *Foreign Affairs* magazine and waiting for her to call, but when she didn't, he began to wonder if he should make the first move. As it so happened, Aunt Bitsy called to ask something about the wedding preparations and he inadvertently let slip that they'd had a spat.

"You must telephone her right away," Aunt Bitsy said.

She explained that Bryce was already remiss in not having apologized last night. "Remiss" was another one of those words he realized he never heard anyone use other than Aunt Bitsy.

He tried to explain that Claudia had insulted him first by suggesting that his tastes were unsophisticated, but she simply said "You'll be a much happier man and have a much happier marriage if you'll resolve right now to always apologize first."

Bryce promised he would call Claudia without delay. He did, and he was glad she accepted his apology, although she didn't offer one of her own. *Maybe she's just too proud*, he reasoned.

Claudia said she was going shopping for underthings at La Perla that afternoon and would catch up with him later.

Bryce felt restless. This time of year could be difficult. The cold and snow seemed to go on forever. The joyful winter holidays had passed, and it would be a long time until Easter. Lent was coming late this year, so he didn't even have that to look forward to.

On an impulse, he decided to drive up to the cabin. It would be even more remote and snowier than Larchmont, but maybe the solitude would be more cozy since it was in the country. He hadn't yet slept there overnight since acquiring the property months ago. He wondered if he were putting it off intentionally. *What am I afraid of, Grandfather's ghost?* he wondered.

Halfway there, he called Rohan. He thought having company would be nice. They could play chess and drink brandy.

"Hi Rohan," said Bryce.

"Well, hello there," Rohan replied.

"I'm on my way up to Norfolk to the cabin. Feel like joining me?" he asked.

"Bryce, I would love to," said Rohan, "Really, I would love to. But I've got to get to the airport this afternoon and fly home. Some wedding preparations require my attention. My mother's already angry that I haven't come earlier. I'm very sorry. I wish I could go."

"Things getting stressful?" Bryce asked.

"Bloody hell—you won't believe what I've been through," Rohan said. He sounded exasperated. "Our traditional weddings are so complicated, you Americans have no idea," he said.

"I know the Jews step on a glass during the ceremony and crush it. Will your fiancée be stepping on a frog?" Bryce hoped to provoke Rohan's laughter.

"Oh, man," said Rohan. "Don't get me started on that girl. She has been so demanding, so incredibly difficult—I don't know how my family has put up with it. Really, I don't. If she were not so rich, I'm telling you, she would be gone. But because her family is so rich, they allow her to get her way. But enough," he said, changing the subject. "How are you doing?"

Bryce realized sadly that Rohan was too stressed even to laugh.

"Not bad. I just felt like getting away for a bit," Bryce said.

"Ah," said Rohan. "Up in the country in Connecticut. You will go and be a hermit, is that it?" Bryce thought he heard the faint stirrings of a giggle coming on in Rohan's voice.

"Yes," said Bryce.

"You'll be killing and eating bears in front of an open fire, right?" Rohan asked. There was definitely a trace of laughter.

"Not quite, but something like that. Maybe marshmallows is more like it," Bryce said.

"Marshmallows! Right! That's it!" Rohan said gleefully. "I hear they congregate in grocery stores. You will hunt them down, right, Bryce? Capture a whole flock of them!" he joked, before erupting into hilarity.

"It takes great skill," Bryce quipped.

"I'd better leave off now so you can stalk your prey." Rohan was absolutely consumed by crazed mirth.

"Okay, have a safe trip," Bryce said.

Before he hung up, he could hear Rohan laughing and saying "The Mighty Marshmallow Hunter of Norfolk, Connecticut!"

26

The cabin was very cold; so cold that it seemed to be even colder indoors than outside. Old buildings had a way of doing that which Bryce never understood.

Every time he'd ever come to the cabin in winter, Grandfather was already there, so it was warm and comfortable. This time, he was the one who'd have to open the place up.

He turned up the heat first and then checked on the food and liquor supplies. He unpacked his clothes.

It was mid-afternoon, so he still had time to run errands before darkness. Maybe he would stop for a cup of tea.

He could go to Colebrook. He liked Colebrook. When he was a little boy, he'd inadvertently amused his parents once as they drove down Main Street by announcing "I think this is where Santa Claus lives." To him, it looked like the North Pole. He fully expected to see little elves emerge from the quaint old buildings or from behind the lamp-posts, all decorated with wreaths.

The most prominent town in the county was further away and he didn't care for the atmosphere. It was very nice, but as Grandfather used to say, it was pretentious. Maybe tomorrow morning he would head up to Great Barrington, across the Massachusetts border, and see what was going on. In nice weather, it was a great place for antiquing.

Bryce remembered one place in particular: a huge old white house with giant columns out front. Its Greek Revival architecture gave it a stately, towering appearance, but the building had clearly seen better days, such as during the Civil War. It was officially known as The Gileses Antiques, but everyone called it "Giles' Junk Shop." He loved going there as a child, although it was both fascinating and frightening.

The building was four stories. On the first floor were the high-end antiques in excellent condition, mostly large expensive pieces of ornate furniture. Up one flight were lamps and small tables and sets of exquisite china, as well as rare *objects d'art*. An uncertain-looking wooden staircase led up a further flight to a third floor filled with a haphazard collection of items: rusty old sets of Chinese checkers missing marbles, broken Victrolas, and ancient tennis rackets. The dirty grey floorboards creaked when stepped upon and everything smelled faintly musty. If anyone dared climb the rickety steps to the fourth floor, which few did, they beheld a badly water-damaged ceiling, cracked window-panes, and a bizarre assembly of cobweb-covered horrors, such as limbless dolls with smashed heads, mangled taxidermy items, and ominous-looking medical instruments used in the days when most people died during surgery. To add to the already unsettling atmosphere, there was a thin path along which one had to walk or risk falling through the rotted floorboards to the flight below. Several holes in the floor marked the areas where unsuspecting visitors had already sent a leg through. Around the time Bryce was a young teen, the fourth floor was permanently cordoned off, forbidden forever to the public.

The most fascinating thing about a visit to Giles' Junk Shop, however, was the hearse. Beside the building was a Victorian horse-drawn hearse. The black carriage rested on enormous thin-spoked wheels. Moth-eaten creamy grey silk curtains festooned the windows and inside lay a real human skeleton, the kind doctors used to display in their offices before plastic was invented.

A small card inscribed in calligraphy with a verse rested against the skeleton's ribs. It read:

As you are now, so once was I
As I am now, so you shall be
So prepare, my friend, and follow me.

Bryce could not forget those lines. The first time that he read them marked the moment that he understood what death actually meant. The skeleton had once been like him, and someday he was going to be like the skeleton. It was the most obvious thing in the world, but everyone pretended it wasn't so. Elaborate social customs, philosophies, and religious niceties were promulgated to create the impression that people lived forever, but they didn't. In fact, Bryce realized with a tinge of fresh horror, the skeleton was already inside him, lying in wait for the day when the rest of him was gone.

Every time he went to Giles' he would stand transfixed, looking at the skeleton and remembering its message for him. Invariably, his parents or Susan would call him away from the macabre artifact, but the memory remained.

At some point in the not-too-distant past, Bryce heard that Giles' had been condemned and torn down, easily a few decades too late, but he was sorry it was gone.

He wished it were summer so he could go to Tanglewood. The concert venue was a convenient drive from the cabin, and he enjoyed picnicking on the lawn while the strains of classical music resounded in the Berkshire valley as twilight fell.

But now was not the time for thinking of summer, he realized. He needed bread and cheese and coffee and a few bottles of wine. He would need fresh vegetables, and the makings of Boeuf Bourguignon.

He headed out to the nearest grocery store, which was in Canaan. They had a limited selection of items, but in an area this secluded, things were apt to be a bit backwards. It was certainly better than the alternative, being overrun with New Money and having gourmet cheese shops on every corner. The *nouveau riche* were always a parody of wealth; they lived the way they imagined the rich did, never realizing that rich people really didn't whip out their credit cards at every opportunity, or turn their noses up at those who served them.

Susan had once related a story about a formal event she'd attended in the city. In the ladies' room, there was a large wicker basket into which hand-towels were to be placed after use. She watched one woman about her age use a towel and then toss it on the floor.

"Excuse me," Susan had sternly remarked, "Your towel didn't make it into the basket."

Answering back over her shoulder, the woman glibly replied "Let the maid pick it up."

Hearing this, the elderly woman who was attending the room registered no emotion. She simply rose from her chair to complete the task, but Susan picked the towel up herself.

Besides their infuriating and disgraceful behavior, the newly rich strove to invoke envy, "putting it all out on the front lawn," as Uncle Clement used to say. They craved the spotlight of media attention, mugging for Patrick McMullan's camera at society events. They had no appreciation of culture. Bryce could hardly think of anything more sickening; they were informal, undisciplined, and gaudy. They were as loathsome as a plague of locusts, and no decent people anywhere welcomed their presence. This is why Grandfather had always told Bryce about the importance of ingratiating himself with the locals. Just because he could buy up a lot of land in a small town didn't mean he had the right to treat other residents poorly. He could certainly advocate for his own interests, but he had to have respect for the common people, most of whom had lived there for generations. Their entitlements had to be considered.

On the drive to Canaan, Bryce considered what an odd place Connecticut was. Grandfather used to say that God created Connecticut because He needed something to fill up the space between Boston and New York. Bryce liked to think of the three states as sisters. Boston was the eldest sister, classically beautiful and profoundly accomplished. New York was the charming youngest sister, brimming with talent, possibility, and vibrant energy. Meanwhile, Connecticut was like the plain middle sister, unremarkable and overlooked. She was outshone by both her sisters and lacked any distinguishing qualities of her own, but there was something touching about her demureness. Connecticut was stoic but dependable. It was the kind of place families like Bryce's had clung to for as long as anyone could remember.

Even the sky was different in Connecticut. Anywhere else in the world, the heavens proclaimed their mood: beaming, as in the Caribbean; temperamental, as in Texas; elucidating, as in Greece, or chilling, as in Norway. The taciturn sky which Bryce beheld revealed nothing. It was inexpressive, never fully bright or darkening.

He drove on.

27

A few days in the country had done him some good. By the time he got back, Claudia was happy to see him. They went for lunch and Bryce picked up the mail in the lobby on the way back into his building. He'd received something from his lawyer.

Upstairs, he opened it and, glancing at a packet of legal papers that the cover letter described as something for his records, he placed them on his desk to be filed away later.

Claudia picked up the papers. She sat on the couch and flipped through the pages while Bryce opened the rest of his mail.

"Bryce," she said. "Who are these from?"

"From Michael," he answered.

"Was Susan the executrix of your grandfather's estate?" she asked.

"Yes," he answered. "Why?"

Claudia showed Bryce a page where Susan had indicated the properties and monies that should be distributed to Bryce, along with the cabin.

"What's unusual about that?" Bryce asked.

"It looks to me like this document is claiming that she owns these things and she's transferring them to you," she explained.

Bryce looked at the page but couldn't make sense of it. "I don't think that's it," he said. "Those things were left to me by Grandfather. This is probably just some legal thing Susan had to sign as executrix."

"I don't think so," Claudia said. She looked through the other pages. "There isn't anything else like this in here. I bet it got put it by mistake."

"Claudia, what are you talking about? How could those things have belonged to Susan? That would mean Grandfather didn't leave me anything." As soon as the words were out of his mouth, his eyes met Claudia's. If her stare were a laser, it would've gone straight through him.

He picked up the phone and called Susan.

28

An hour later, Bryce sat staring out the window, speechless with disbelief. Claudia had been right. Grandfather hadn't left Bryce a dime.

"Patty and I discussed it," Susan explained. "We were both in complete agreement that I should give you a share."

"But he didn't want me to have anything?" Bryce had asked, incredulous. "Not even a keepsake? What the hell did the man think of me?"

"That's not the issue," Susan protested.

"What did I ever do to him?" he asked. "I wasn't his favorite, but I never disrespected him or caused him harm."

"Bryce," Susan began.

"No, Susan, I'm not going to listen to you talk me in circles," he said.

"You're obviously wounded right now, and that's to be expected," she said.

"Damn right, I'm feeling wounded," he shot back. The more he thought about it, the more upset he became. "What exactly did Grandfather say to you about me?"

They had quibbled for several more minutes until finally Susan knew Bryce would not be satisfied unless he had the truth. She took a deep breath.

"This is painful for me to tell you, I want you to know that," she began.

"Fine. Point made. Now tell me," he demanded.

Susan went on to explain that Grandfather had predicted from the very beginning that Bryce wouldn't be much use to the family and therefore, being a shrewd businessman, didn't bother investing much time in him. Susan was quick to add that she didn't believe Grandfather had any particular affection for her, but that he favored her simply because she was more compliant and seemed to fall into step with his ideals. She went on to say that Bryce's distancing himself from the family was something Grandfather found absolutely unforgiveable.

"If you must know, he used to call it a slap in the face," she said.

"What?" Bryce exclaimed. "What I did was nothing against him—it was never meant to hurt him. How could he possibly take it that way?"

"Because there is no such thing as individual choices in a family like ours. You're either with us, or you're not. You know this," she said.

"Sure," he retorted, "I know I'm not allowed to become a movie star or write a tell-all book or marry the town whore, but why can't I just quietly go live my own life? I wasn't hurting anybody."

"Of course you were, Bryce. Do I have to spell it out for you?" she said tiredly.

"Yes, Susan, please. Please spell away. Tell me how I became Charles Manson."

"What do you think we had to tell people when they asked after you? What do you think it was like for the rest of us when you weren't keeping up your responsibilities? How embarrassed do you think we were when everyone started marrying their daughters off to your peers because you weren't even a consideration?" she asked.

“You weren’t either,” he sneered.

“That’s not the same. I never turned my back on my family. Patty is one of us,” she explained. “Even Grandfather realized that who I am wasn’t going to weaken our stability. Society can expand enough to accept me, Bryce, but not you,” she said, her voice now ragged with hurt.

“So you mean I’m the one who killed society? Quick, someone call Cleveland Amory!” he said.

The rest of the conversation did not go well. Bryce ended the call shortly when he realized he was too angry to continue. Claudia left soon after, so Bryce could have some time to himself.

So the old man hated my guts, he thought.

The sting of his disinheritance was indescribable. It was a punishment, a very punitive punishment, designed by a coldhearted man in a position of authority to make him feel very small. It was the action of a person who saw the world strictly in terms of black and white.

Of course, Bryce realized that had Grandfather not seen the world in those terms and had he not been coldhearted, the family fortune would never have flourished, so it was a two-edged sword, and it drew malicious cuts on its victims.

Thanks to Susan’s charity (which other relatives—if they knew about it—would probably consider misguided) he’d have something to make his life easier and a door would be left ajar for him to reunite with his own kind, but what about the years that intervened? Was Claudia whispered about behind her back for marrying “that crazy Bryce Parnell”? Did people shun Deek for having stood by him all those years? He was drowning in a mental flood of negative possibilities. It was like seeing his face on the “Wanted” list at the post office and not understanding why.

He went for a long run until he was too tired to think any more. Then he had a light supper and retired for the evening, feeling worse than he had in a long time.

29

When he awoke, Bryce remembered the jarring news of the previous day. He felt strangely liberated, as though something that had bound him was suddenly gone. He realized that perhaps his feelings of obligation to the family and to Grandfather had weighed on him in the consideration of personal matters, and now that he knew Grandfather had utterly disowned him, that obligation had dissolved.

As he had his morning coffee and toast, he reflected that it was entirely possible to reframe his relationship to his family as one of possibility, but not necessarily one of responsibility. There were certain indelible benefits to bearing the Parnell name; courtesies that would be afforded him, and leverage that could be invoked. On the other hand, he was free to live his life as he wished. Should Susan—or anyone in his circle—attempt to recriminate him for not behaving in a certain way, the truth of the matter was that his “membership” in the family had been withdrawn by Grandfather.

If Grandfather's will were widely known, Bryce reasoned, no one could expect anything of him, other than not creating some kind of scandal or otherwise bringing unspeakable shame upon the family.

It was a good thought, a freeing thought.

The only problem with it, Bryce realized, was that Claudia's fate was tied to his, and he guessed she would not be in agreement with his assessment of things. In fact, she would probably suggest that Bryce's obligation to his family was that much more imperative, given that he had been included by the skin of his teeth (and Susan's good grace). Claudia would undoubtedly say that he should work even harder to secure his place and that of their children.

Bryce rubbed his temples. This kind of strategizing drained him. It wasn't that he couldn't come up with answers, it was just that he didn't like the answers he came up with. Breaking his engagement with Claudia would free him completely, and allow her to find someone who could give her the kind of future she wanted.

Bryce knew this was too big a decision to be made all at once. He told himself he would wait it out for a few months and see how things transpired.

30

By the time spring arrived and the first purple crocus pushed its way out of the snow, Bryce was in an optimistic mood.

To be sure, nothing had changed. He'd continued to observe wedding plans from as much of a distance as he could manage. He and Claudia had attended several charity balls, some of which were enjoyable, and several of Claudia's work-related arts events, which were excruciating.

Claudia herself had not changed, although she did pressure Bryce to keep step with their social responsibilities. The one point on which they had not yet reconciled was Claudia's suggestion that he contact Cricket and set things right with his club membership, which he steadfastly refused to do. Nevertheless, he had a feeling Claudia was going to keep at him about it in hopes of eventually wearing him down.

Still, something about spring made him happy. He had continued to find ways to use his newfound wealth and connections to his benefit, picking up a few good investment opportunities and doing a bit of beneficial networking.

Susan and Patty invited Bryce and Claudia for Easter dinner, but they had to refuse as they were going instead to Claudia's brother's house in Oyster Bay. Susan told Bryce that Patty had finally forgiven him for his outburst on Christmas, and he was glad of that.

One Sunday morning when Claudia was out with friends, he received a call from a number he didn't recognize.

"Bryce," said the caller, "It's Stephanie."

Bryce was surprised. "Hello—how are you?"

"I'm fine. I got your number from Susan."

"Is everything okay?" Bryce asked. Whenever someone called unexpectedly, he knew there was a good chance there was bad news to be shared.

"Yes, I suppose so," she said.

Bryce sensed her response was definitely a harbinger of bad news yet to come. "How's Topher?" he asked.

"In the hospital—but he'll be fine," she quickly added.

"What happened?" Bryce asked.

"Actually, I was calling to see if you'd like to get together sometime," Stephanie said. "I know it's been a long time and I'd love to catch up with you."

"That sounds wonderful," said Bryce. "Are you free now? I'll take you to brunch."

"Okay," Stephanie agreed.

They met an hour later at a place in Hartsdale.

Bryce hadn't seen Stephanie in at least ten years. She still looked the same, although her honey-colored hair was darker and her figure was leaner and more toned. Overall, he decided he probably liked her better. There was something more mature about her that he found appealing, and she was still as bright and congenial as ever.

Sitting across from Stephanie, Bryce felt that they had picked up exactly where they had left off years before.

After exchanging a few niceties, Stephanie explained what led up to her current circumstances. Topher had started behaving strangely a few years back. She didn't think anything of it, not sure what it meant. There had been a few car accidents, but she had chalked it up to Topher's notoriously poor driving skills. Bryce, for his part, chalked it up to Topher's overall stupidity, but either way, it didn't matter.

Eventually, Stephanie had become suspicious that something was amiss. In a desperate act very unlike her, she eavesdropped on one of Topher's private phone calls and discovered that he was arranging for someone to pick up drugs for him.

"What kind of drugs?" Bryce asked.

"Pills and cocaine," Stephanie said.

Bryce was shocked. Topher didn't seem like a pills and cocaine kind of guy. Then again, he was stupid, so Bryce could see how he could easily fall into any kind of trouble.

"It turns out he was suffering from low self-esteem," Stephanie was explaining. "He wasn't happy in his work," she said.

After years of laboring at difficult jobs for pitiful wages, Bryce didn't have a lot of sympathy for Topher's plight as a figurehead executive who probably spent his day doing crossword puzzles, if he were even bright enough to know how.

"The drugs made him feel good about himself," Stephanie was saying. She told Bryce that Topher had tried several methods for getting off drugs during the ensuing months, but suffered multiple relapses. Finally, his doctor recommended that he go to rehab.

"So that's where he is now?" Bryce asked.

"Yes," Stephanie said. "It's been very difficult for me, but I'm glad to know he's getting the help he needs," she said.

"Yes, that's important," said Bryce.

Stephanie spoke frankly about her worries, the strain caused by Topher's addiction, and her uncertainty about the future.

"I've been seeing a therapist," Stephanie continued, "who thinks that at a time like this, I need to expand my social support network. He said I should connect with people who make me feel good about myself, and you were always one of those people, which is why I called."

Bryce was flattered. He figured that after having broken her heart, he'd be one of the last people she'd want to be around.

"I'm sorry I never got back in touch; to be honest, I didn't think you'd want to hear from me," he said.

"No, I'm sorry I didn't contact you sooner," Stephanie said. "There were so many times over the years when I would've loved to get in touch, but I didn't know if you'd want to talk to me."

"Of course I'd want to talk to you, Stephanie," Bryce said. "You've always meant a lot to me."

"Really?" she asked.

"Yes," he said.

Their conversation changed to happier things and touched on the little details of their current lives. Bryce watched in fascination as Stephanie had trouble getting forkfuls of scrambled egg into her mouth. Little bits of egg kept falling out the sides. It had always been one of her personal etiquette failings. Like all people raised with good manners, her manners weren't entirely perfect. In fact, Bryce could always tell someone who hadn't been born rich because their manners were impeccable, owing to having been recently acquired. It was similar to the way converts always knew a religion better than those born into it. One of the things Bryce always found amusing about attending cocktail parties with Stephanie was the way that canapes always fell out of the sides of her mouth. She'd get most of one in, and even make fervent chomping motions to devour it whole, but part of a cracker or a pinch of rosemary or a bit of cream cheese or *something* would invariably fall out one side. It was interesting to watch.

"I would've loved to have taken you to brunch at the St. Moritz, but it doesn't exist anymore," Bryce said sadly.

"I know!" Stephanie rejoined, a bit of egg escaping from the corner of her mouth and tumbling to her plate. "Can you believe it? It's just heartbreaking."

"We should go to the city," Bryce suddenly said, on a whim.

Stephanie smiled at him. "Okay," she said.

Bryce paid the tab and they left. He drove them to the train station and they arrived in Grand Central shortly afterwards.

"How about drinks at the Algonquin?" he suggested.

"Love it!" Stephane said.

While neither of them were great drinkers or partiers, something about the moment lent itself to the oblivion of drinking. Before they knew it, they'd consumed several cocktails on top of the mimosas they'd had with brunch. They ordered some tea around 3PM just to put the brakes on, and split a club sandwich, but after that they left in search of somewhere else to sit and drink.

As they walked along West 44th Street, Stephanie linked her arm in his. He smiled at her. Acting on an impulse, a few paces later, he led her into a doorway out of the current of passers-by and kissed her. When he stepped back, they were both out of breath.

"I want you," Stephanie said.

Bryce took her hand. "Come on," he said, leading her down the street.

"Aren't you going to say something?" Stephanie asked.

"We can't do this," Bryce said. "We shouldn't do this."

"I know, but I want to anyway. Does that make me a bad person?"

"I don't know," Bryce answered.

The walked in silence for another few blocks. Before they knew it, they were in Hell's Kitchen. Stephanie spied a small bar with a Spanish name on a side street, and they went in.

The walls were whitewashed with ornate inset tiles and a few old men were drinking at the bar and speaking Spanish. Bryce and Stephanie sat down and the bartender asked them what they wanted. Bryce ordered a pitcher of sangria.

"I feel like a couple of outlaws," Stephanie said with a grin.

"Well, at least no one will recognize us here," Bryce said.

They laughed and talked for almost an hour. The bartender smiled at them.

"You a very nice couple," he said.

They thanked him. Some of the old men at the bar also turned and nodded their heads approvingly.

The bartender addressed Bryce. “When you going to marry this beautiful woman?”

Bryce and Stephanie exchanged glances. The old men waited to see what Bryce would say.

“Maybe someday,” Bryce said.

The old men grumbled and spoke in Spanish amongst themselves.

“Listen, friend,” said the bartender, “you have a beautiful woman like this, my advice is—don’t wait.”

Stephanie giggled.

A little while later they left.

“Where are we going now?” Stephanie asked.

“We’re going back to Grand Central and getting on the train to Hartsdale, then I’m driving you home,” he said.

“Okay,” said Stephanie.

Along the way they kissed again in the street, several times.

Before they could make it to Grand Central Station, they checked into a hotel.

31

It was almost 7:30PM when Bryce woke up. Stephanie was asleep next to him in bed. He shook her gently.

“What is it?” she asked sleepily.

“It’s seven-thirty. Don’t you have to be home?” he asked with concern.

“Topher’s in rehab,” she said. “He won’t know where I am.” She rolled over.

Bryce looked at the back of Stephanie’s head. He reached over and petted her hair. When they were young, they had dated for almost a year without being intimate, yet today, just a few short hours after reuniting, they’d slept together despite each being involved in other relationships.

Life was strange.

Bryce got up and got dressed. He checked his phone; no messages from Claudia.

Stephanie began stirring. She got up and pulled her clothes on.

“What have we done?” Bryce asked.

“I’m not sure, but I don’t feel bad about it,” Stephanie said.

"You're the one who has the most to lose here," Bryce said. "If Topher ever found out, he could divorce you."

"I don't know that'd I'd be too upset about that," Stephanie said. "Things have been difficult these last few years. I didn't tell you before, but Topher hired this financial manager who had no idea what he was doing and lost us a lot of money."

"I didn't know that," Bryce said.

"Bryce, I haven't been that happy with Topher. I've suffered. It's time that I take stock of my life and make decisions based on love, not on fear," she said. Bryce figured she was quoting her therapist.

"I married Topher because I was afraid of being single and I wanted children," she said. "then it turned out that we couldn't have them anyway."

"I'm sorry," Bryce offered.

"But don't you see? Look where my decision has led. I'm lonely and I realize that marrying him was a mistake," she said. "What about you?" she asked. "Do you love Claudia?"

"Of course," Bryce said spontaneously.

"I don't believe that or you wouldn't be here right now," Stephanie said.

"Even if I weren't in love with her, she doesn't deserve this," he said. "She'd never do anything like this to me."

"Bryce, maybe this isn't about living according to some code of honor, maybe it's about living from a place of authenticity," she said. Bryce knew a phrase like that had to have come from a therapist.

"What do you mean?" he asked.

"I care for Topher, but our marriage is over," she said. "It's horrible for me to say that, but it's the truth. It's also true that I have feelings for you." She paused a moment. "Do you have feelings for me?"

"Yes, but I have an obligation to Claudia," he said.

"I agree, Bryce, but maybe your obligation to her is to be honest with her," she said. "I'm not asking you to leave her for me, but I'm suggesting you look at this from her point of view. Do you think she wants to be married to someone who doesn't love her?"

"That's not the kind of question I can answer," he said, thinking of how Aunt Bitsy had laid out Claudia's predicament after her first engagement fell through. "She wants to have a life with me. I know that."

Stephanie came over to Bryce and kissed him. They gathered their things and left the hotel.

32

Despite telling himself on the way home that he would never sleep with Stephanie again, and resolving that he would never tell Claudia about what had happened in order to spare her feelings, Bryce was elated when Stephanie called a few days later.

Since the afternoon of their tryst, Bryce had come to look on the situation as his own personal spy game. It was an exciting, secret part of his life. At first, it had just been a memory of an afternoon when he had lost himself to passion, but he had to admit that the thought had occurred to him that he could continue seeing Stephanie as long as she were willing, which she appeared to be.

They went to the cinema, and then out for dinner at a nearby Japanese restaurant. Bryce was afraid they'd be recognized. He realized that returning to either of their residences would be unwise, and then he remembered the cabin. They planned to spend the next weekend there together. Nobody ever came to visit him there because they knew he didn't live there, and while the locals recognized him, they wouldn't know anyone who was with him.

As for his guilt, he reconciled it by saying that maybe he would break off the engagement with Claudia. There was still time, as the wedding wasn't to take place until September. After all, that's what an engagement was, wasn't it—an opportunity to make a final decision about whether or not to go through with the marriage? Better that he should take advantage of this opportunity to be sure than to remain forever undecided.

It was a kind of free-fall situation, which was rare in Bryce's life.

Just see what happens, he told himself.

33

The arrangement worked well. Bryce and Stephanie continued to spend time together at the cabin, but they frequently talked on the phone during the week, too. Theirs was as much a friendship as a romance.

Topher had been scheduled to leave rehab at the end of the month, but he had been caught with drugs, so it was agreed that his stay was extended. For once, Bryce was grateful for Topher's stupidity.

Stephanie told Bryce that her parents wanted her to remain married to him, but Stephanie said, "It's not like there are children involved, and at this point I have more money than he does, so it hardly makes sense."

"They're just thinking of your best interests," Bryce suggested.

"No, they're afraid of the stigma of having a divorced daughter," Stephanie said. "I don't blame them, but I have to live my life on my own terms." Bryce was sure that gem had come from her therapist.

Bryce wished he felt as sure of himself as Stephanie did. Claudia was busy with wedding plans and work, so the affair didn't affect their relationship at all, and if she suspected anything, she certainly didn't show it. However, from time to time he would become anxious, wondering how everything would end up. But then he would let himself lapse back into the enjoyment of the moment.

He realized he and Stephanie wouldn't be able to spend Easter together, which made him sad. The year they were dating, he'd made up a little Easter basket for her, filled with candies and a few pairs of earrings. She was crazy about tangerine Life Savers, so he'd bought a roll of those and taped a paper bunny's head, which he'd drawn and cut out, to one end of the pack and a cotton ball to the other end.

They talked a lot about old times. She made him remember so many good things from the past; things that no longer existed.

"Where did it all go?" Bryce once asked her.

"I think our way of life was dying even then, but we didn't know it," Stephanie replied.

Later that week, Bryce stopped by Aunt Bitsy's to discuss some of his mother's jewelry which he was going to give to Claudia as a wedding present. Aunt Bitsy knew exactly what Mother had intended for whom, so she wanted to make her recommendations to Bryce.

When he arrived, he found her mildly agitated, which was unusual.

"I've just been lunching with the most odious woman," she said. "She belongs to one of the foundations with which I'm connected," she explained. "Or rather," she said, correcting herself, "Perhaps I should say she doesn't belong."

"New money?" Bryce asked.

Aunt Bitsy nodded. "Yes, she wears those tacky things from Talbot's because she thinks it's refined. But it's not just her lack of taste," she qualified, "she has no real interest in the work we're doing. It's dreadful."

"Can I ask you something, Aunt Bitsy?" Bryce asked.

"Certainly, dear," she said with concern.

"What happens to people like us in the end?" He knew he didn't have to explain what he meant because he knew she already knew.

"Bryce," she said, "The reason we are who we are is because generations ago, people who were poor and cold and hungry decided they wanted something better for themselves and their children. All the captains of industry came from nothing, and they left behind empires. They valued education and culture, and they even sought to improve the lives of the common people. Of course, over time, poor choices and dwindling opportunities have brought some families to reduced circumstances, and the influx of the newly rich has diminished our presence in society.

But Bryce," she assured him, "nothing can change who you are and the fact that you come from people who have always held high standards, regardless of anything else."

"I know," Bryce said.

She told him, "There's a difference between being flexible and surrendering. The tallest trees in the forest are there because they bend with the wind when a fierce storm comes, but as soon as it passes, they go right back to standing straight up the way they did before."

Bryce was somewhat heartened by Aunt Bitsy's tenacity, yet she hadn't really answered his question. He also noted she'd left out some important facts in her version of how the captains of industry came into being—facts about underhanded business deals, worker oppression, and tax evasion. She probably knew about that, he reasoned, but overall, it didn't change her point about the old families.

Regardless, even if they bent with the wind and held the standard aloft, Bryce knew that ultimately, they were doomed.

He left Aunt Bitsy's having agreed to give Mother's diamond earrings, diamond necklace, and sapphire brooch to Claudia on their wedding day.

34

The following week, he met Stephanie for lunch in Scarsdale. There was an errand he had to run in the area and he hoped anyone who saw them would assume they were just two old friends, which, in essence, they were.

As he went to help her out of her car, he saw a small stack of magazines on the passenger side.

"When did you start reading *The Atlantic*?" he asked.

"Oh, those are for Topher. I'm going to the hospital after lunch," she said.

Bryce considered *The Atlantic* a publication for those who weren't intelligent enough to understand *The New Yorker*, so he wasn't the least surprised to learn that Topher read it.

Over lunch, as Bryce watched wayward leaves of lettuce from Stephanie's sandwich struggle free from the corners of her mouth and flutter to her plate below, he had to ask himself what he had gotten himself involved in. The situation between them could not continue. Topher would be out of rehab soon. Bryce didn't want to be a catalyst for Stephanie leaving her husband. His own marriage would take place in several months.

"I'm thinking of talking to my lawyer," Stephanie said. "It's just scary for me to make things so final."

"I wouldn't do anything hasty if I were you," Bryce counseled.

"But I know what I want," she said. "I'll be much better off without him. And then there's us," she added.

Bryce looked up from his cream of asparagus soup. "How do you mean?" he asked.

"I'm not asking you for anything, Bryce, but I need to tell you how I feel," she began. "I love you and I want to be with you. I'm not suggesting you leave Claudia—unless you want to, of course—but no matter how we figure out how to do it, I'd like to maintain a relationship."

"So you'll leave Topher and you want to continue seeing me whether I'm single or married?" Bryce asked.

"Yes," Stephanie said. "I've been in love with you since we were young. You were the one I should've married, but that's the past. We can do things differently now. I just want to be completely honest with you."

Bryce paused before answering. "There's a lot to consider," he said. "I don't think it would be right or good for us to keep seeing each other after I marry Claudia."

"What if you didn't marry her? I'm not suggesting you shouldn't, just being hypothetical," she said.

"Then we'd both be single," Bryce said.

"Right," agreed Stephanie.

"And there is always the possibility of remarriage," Bryce conceded, although he didn't know how he felt about marrying a divorcée.

"You would consider it?" Stephanie asked hopefully.

"Of course," Bryce replied, but he still wasn't sure.

"We could always just live together," Stephanie offered.

Bryce looked down at his soup. Before he'd even had the chance to take another spoonful, the conversation had gone from Stephanie thinking of leaving Topher to talk of him dissolving his engagement to Claudia and living with Stephanie. *This is moving too fast for me*, he realized.

"I don't know if I like the idea of living together," he stated.

"That's only one possible scenario," Stephanie said.

'Scenario'? Now we're talking about scenarios? Bryce thought.

"We could continue to keep our own residences and still have a relationship," Stephanie suggested. "It could be very informal."

The word "informal" triggered Bryce's realization of the source of his discomfort with the conversation. Everything they were discussing was non-traditional; they would be winging it, off-roading, flying by the seat of their pants.

"I think that's exactly what I don't like about the idea," Bryce said.

"Oh," Stephanie said, "Then you'd want to marry me?"

"No," Bryce said flatly. "I think the whole thing has run its course and it's time for us to get on with our lives."

Stephanie looked at Bryce with a blank expression.

Bryce went to take her hand in his, but remembering they were in public, he put his hands back in his lap.

"Listen," he said, "I care about you very much and what we've had has been wonderful. I've never done anything like this in my life, and I have to admit, it was extremely exhilarating. I've completely enjoyed every moment we've spent together, but we knew it couldn't last. You have Topher to get back to and I have Claudia."

"But you said you have feelings for me," Stephanie protested.

"I do," Bryce said, "But there are other factors. You need to be there for Topher."

"No, I don't," Stephanie said. "Haven't you been listening to me for the past two months? I've been explaining that I think I want to leave him."

"Be that as it may," Bryce continued, "I have a wedding coming up and I don't think it would be right to disappoint Claudia."

Stephanie took his words in. "I wouldn't mind it if you said you didn't want me because you love Claudia, or because you didn't want to be the reason I left Topher, but you admitted you have feelings for me and you know I'm going to leave Topher anyway—how can you sit there and tell me that it's over between us?" she asked.

"Because it is" Bryce said.

"But it doesn't have to be," Stephanie said emphatically. "We can make this whatever we want. I'm willing to work with you so it's something we're both comfortable with."

"Really, Stephanie, this has gone too far," Bryce said.

"You said you have feelings for me," she whispered.

"Stephanie, it's not that easy, and you know it as well as I do," Bryce said.

They were silent. Bryce saw Stephanie quickly wipe a tear away from the corner of her eye.

When they had finished their lunch and were outside, Bryce said, "It was good to see you and I hope things go well with Topher. You know you can always call me if you need to talk."

"Thanks," Stephanie said, nodding. "I've got a lot to keep me busy. I'm sure you do, too."

"Yes, Claudia's dragging me to a cake-tasting this weekend and we still have about a dozen CDs from different string quartets that we have to listen to so we can decide which one to hire," Bryce said.

"Well then," Stephanie said, her voice suddenly breaking, "I'd better be off." She smiled a tight smile as her eyes filled with tears and she quickly got into her car.

Bryce waved, then turned and headed for his car, which was about a half a block from the restaurant. As he drove away, he saw she hadn't yet left. She was leaning forward in her seat, her head resting on her hands on the steering wheel. He thought about going back to talk to her, but he didn't want to upset her any more than he already had.

35

The clean break from the affair with Stephanie meant that Bryce had more time to devote to Claudia. He threw himself into wedding planning, making helpful suggestions and offering opinions. They also talked about the future.

"Do you think 'Hunter' is a good name for a girl?" Claudia asked, adding, "I'm not sure how I feel about it."

"I think it sounds pompous," Bryce said.

"My mother's maiden name was Gardiner. That could be pretty," she said.

"Maybe," Bryce said. "I've always liked 'Nigel' for a boy."

On impulse, Bryce asked her "How about we go up to the cabin this weekend?"

Claudia explained that she couldn't, as she already had plans with her mother and nieces, something to do with them being flower-girls.

Later that same day, Bryce received a call from Susan. She informed him that Minty Masterson was dead.

"Minty?" Bryce had exclaimed with surprise, "What happened?"

Susan explained that Minty had been having various complaints for some time, but the doctors couldn't find anything. At one point, several months ago, they did find what they believed to be the cause. He'd been kept in the hospital for a few days for treatment and released with a clean bill of health. Then he unexpectedly collapsed the previous night at a party for Ben's family, who'd flown over from China for a visit.

"So they still don't know what killed him?" Bryce asked.

"No. Ingrid's having an autopsy done, but his doctor thinks it's probably a type of very rapidly spreading cancer," Susan said.

"How is Ingrid?" Bryce asked.

"Patty and I were there this morning as soon as she called," Susan explained. "She's doing very well, so is Nathalie. Ben's pretty broken up, though. I guess he'd become pretty fond of Minty."

"Oh, that's right, and they've got Ben's parents as well. Are they staying—" Bryce began.

Susan interrupted him. "No, they're in a hotel in the city. They wanted to do the tourist thing since this was their first trip to the states. We invited them to dinner with us tonight so they wouldn't feel—you know—since Ingrid's not up to it, but apparently they're fine on their own."

"I can't believe it, poor old Minty," Bryce said.

"The wake will be held as soon as the autopsy's over, so that's still in the air, but Ingrid's planning the funeral for early next week, probably Tuesday," Susan said.

Bryce heard a voice in the background, and then Susan said, "I have to go. Ingrid's maid's here to pick up some silver we're loaning them for the get-together after the funeral. Take care."

Bryce hung up and sighed. It was sad losing Minty; he was such a staple of their circle, with his larger-than-life presence, booming voice, and trove of amusing stories.

He realized with a pang that Nathalie must be heartbroken. He reached for the phone to call her, but then, remembering she had a fiancé, thought better of the idea. Had she been single, he would've called, but since she already had someone to officially comfort her, it might be a bit awkward for him to contact her. He'd see her at the wake.

36

Bryce and Claudia entered the funeral home, which was packed with mourners. Minty's farewell was going to be the social event of the season, Bryce realized with slight amusement. Minty probably would've liked that.

They said hello to various friends and acquaintances and proceeded to view the body. It seemed strange to Bryce to see Minty so still. He looked good for a dead man, but tired.

Claudia spotted Patty across the room and they made their way over to her. They hugged in greeting. Patty said Susan was in the rest room. They commented on the large crowd. Moments later, Susan appeared. Her eyes were red-rimmed. Bryce guessed that seeing Minty dead was difficult for her. As tough as she tried to be, she took things hard.

They spoke for a few moments and then went to offer their condolences to Ingrid.

Ingrid seemed well. She wore a demure black dress, but was otherwise her usual self. She greeted them warmly and thanked them for coming. She made a few cheerful remarks about how pleased Minty would have been to have so many friends in attendance. Then she changed the subject to their wedding and she and Claudia spoke for several minutes about that. Finally, a fresh wave of mourners arrived and were headed towards her, so Bryce and Claudia excused themselves and sought out Nathalie.

"She's holding up very well," Claudia commented to Bryce.

"Yes, that's Ingrid," he said.

They finally found Nathalie ensconced by her former sorority sisters and other college friends in the far corner of the room. Ben stood beside her, holding a cup of water and some tissues. She put her arms out to him as soon as she saw Bryce. He gave her a quick hug.

"Thank you so much for coming," she said sweetly. "I'm so glad to see you."

Bryce introduced Claudia to her and the two made the usual remarks about being sorry they had to meet under such circumstances.

Nathalie looked very drained, but there were only the faintest traces of swelling around her eyes. She didn't look as hale as Ingrid, but she looked fine. Bryce greeted Ben, who seemed very downcast, and introduced him to Claudia.

As Claudia chatted politely with Nathalie and her friends, Bryce realized sadly that Nathalie wouldn't have a father at her wedding. That would be a shame. He wondered who would give her away.

He spoke with Ben briefly about his parents' visit, and asked after them. Ben's father had combined the social visit with some business he had in the city, so between that and touring around, they had a lot to keep them occupied in the absence of family time with the Mastersons, although they were arriving at the wake later in the evening. Ben mentioned that his mother and Nathalie had been getting along very well.

Overhearing this, Nathalie joined the conversation. "I love her," she said. "I absolutely love her. We'd talked on the phone and so we knew each other a little bit but now that she's here, I don't even want her to go back to China!" Ben brightened a little when he heard this. Nathalie turned to him and said "Ben, tell your parents I'm keeping them. Tell them to buy a house in Tuxedo and bring all their friends from China and just stay here." She giggled and her friends laughed. "Why not?" she asked. "We should totally do that."

Bryce and Claudia moved on, greeting a few more people he knew. They stopped for a moment to chat with the Jorgensens.

"What a tragic turn of events," said Aris somberly. "We were all together just a few months ago."

"It's quite sad," Loretta added. "It makes you realize the value of every moment because we never know what will happen next."

Aris explained that they had tickets for some concert a month hence which they had planned to attend with the Mastersons, and they were glad now that it would be an opportunity to take Ingrid out, as she'd told them she would still like to go.

"It's good to keep as much normal activity going as possible," Loretta explained. Aris nodded in agreement.

The Jorgensens were very pleased to meet Claudia and made her promise to tell them all about her grant work some other time. Bryce surmised that was the kind of subject that they would find utterly fascinating.

About thirty minutes later, they left. The crush of people was becoming annoying; they could barely move, but they managed to make it out the door.

37

The funeral, held three days later, was more sparsely attended, unsurprisingly, but still boasted an impressive crowd, Bryce thought. Minty had a lot of business associates and he was a friendly guy.

Ingrid looked sad but dignified. Nathalie sobbed openly a few times, but was otherwise okay. Ben was steely. Bryce saw the people he presumed were Ben's parents next to him in the pew. His father was a handsome man wearing an exceptionally well-tailored coat. Ben's mother was short and pudgy with a fancy hairdo. She was plainly dressed, but wore a lot of rings featuring large colorful stones.

The men carrying Minty's coffin out of the church were tall, Bryce realized as they walked past the row where he and Claudia were sitting. Then again, everyone was tall, thought Bryce, in a congregation of wealthy people. Like horses, they were bred for certain traits, and height was a prime commodity. Bryce tried to think of any important corporate figure he'd ever met who was under 6'2" and he couldn't bring to mind a single one.

Everyone knew tall people were apt to be more successful in society due to prehistoric wiring making everyone think that the bigger and stronger someone was, the more powerful of a leader they would be. Claudia told Bryce that people were even giving their children hormone injections to boost their height, which he found disconcerting, but he didn't doubt it was true. The rich did whatever they could to gain advantages.

As they walked along the sidewalk outside the church past the hearse, Bryce was struck with the realization that Minty was now among the ranks of the dead, just like the occupant of the hearse at Giles' Junk Shop. Someday, all that would be left of Minty would be a skeleton. Such a frail frame wouldn't suit him, though, Bryce thought. Maybe they should bury him with a non-biodegradable hat or a solid gold cane or something. Minty deserved to be distinctive after death.

Back at the Masterson's house, Margaret let them in. Susan had allowed Ingrid to borrow her to help Polly, the Masterson's maid, since so many mourners would be coming. Bryce remembered that Polly made the best shrimp cocktails he'd ever had. She used little shrimps and lots of horseradish in the sauce.

The dining room had been transformed into a large buffet, punctuated by gorgeous flower arrangements. Bryce could smell the inviting scent of hot coffee brewing in the kitchen.

Gradually, the house filled with guests, and the crowd became lively.

Uncle Clement and Aunt fluff arrived. They came over to meet Claudia.

"It's good to have fresh blood in the family now that us old folks are dying off," Uncle Clement said.

"Especially someone so accomplished," Aunt Fluff added. "I think you and Bryce will make a successful team." She smiled her wan smile.

Uncle Clement looked around the room, mentally appraising the contents. "I'm sure Ingrid will be well provided for, especially with that new son-in-law of hers."

"I think the Chinese are so clever, don't you?" Aunt Fluff said. "They're like the Jews, but so much nicer."

Bryce felt his stomach become tense. "Most Jews I've ever met are very nice people," he said.

"Oh, I'm not saying they're not," she clarified. "One of the ladies I worked with for years on a charity committee was a Jewess. Elana Aranoff was her name. She was a lovely person; we treated her just like one of us."

Claudia and Aunt Fluff began a conversation about the committee. Bryce excused himself under the pretense of having to get something he'd accidentally left in his car.

Outside, he took a deep breath. He wanted to get in his car and drive and keep driving. He knew he couldn't, but for a moment, he wondered what it would be like to be someone else. Outside Tuxedo Park was a whole world; a world Bryce had the time and means to explore.

An idea began to take hold. *What if I try restructuring everything?* he thought. He reflected that his finances were in order, the cabin was repaired, and his wedding plans were being more than competently seen to by Claudia. Maybe he could use the time between now and September to do something important and meaningful.

He glanced back at the house. The world of Old Money with its prejudices and entitlements could be wearing, he thought, considering he'd seen another side of life: one in which he had to struggle and suffer. He saw the consequences of choosing not to accept a life that came with strings attached.

In a way, he thought, *I'm a traitor to my class, just like FDR; just like Cleveland Amory.*

Suddenly, he had an inspiration. He would follow Cleveland Amory's example: he would use his money to create something that was the antithesis of everything for which his family stood.

He began to get chilly, so he knew he'd have to go back inside, but this new idea made him feel hopeful. For once, he felt like he was headed in the right direction.

He went back inside and joined Claudia.

38

The next morning, Bryce called Deek.

"I have something to tell you," Bryce said.

"Well, I have something to tell you," Deek replied. "Tiffany and I got engaged last night."

Bryce was somewhat stunned. He knew Deek dated girls like Tiffany but so far, he hadn't ever talked about marrying any of them.

"That's great news," Bryce said automatically.

They spoke for a little while about the event, mostly about how Deek planned to integrate Tiffany into his family. He'd decided on a gradual approach.

"I'm sure Mom and Daddy would be happy to have her out to the island for some events this spring and summer. It's all informal, so I think she'll feel comfortable and it'll give her a chance to get used to us," he explained.

Bryce thought the whole idea was ludicrous, but he wanted to be supportive of Deek. "I'm sure everything will work out," he said.

Deek asked Bryce what his news was, so Bryce told him.

"You know how I never quite fit in with the family; well, I've been thinking a lot about Cleveland Amory and how he bucked tradition by using his inheritance to start a ranch for unwanted animals," he said.

"Cleveland Amory? I knew he wrote some books—something about a cat—but I never heard about this ranch," Deek said.

"It's down in Texas, and I want to go there. And I want you to go with me. It'll be a road trip," Bryce suggested.

"A road trip to Texas?" Deek said. "Look, I hate to say no to you, Bryce, but right now isn't a really good time."

"Come on, Deek," Bryce said. "It'll be great. Just the two of us."

"Honestly, I can't. There's a lot going on right now," Deek said.

"Well," Bryce conceded, "I guess I'll just go alone then, but if you change your mind, you can always call me."

"I will," Deek said. "Have a safe trip and tell me all about it when you get back."

Bryce sent Claudia an e-mail telling her about the trip, basically saying that he wanted to visit a ranch in Texas that Amory founded and that he wouldn't be gone long and that it was a spur of the moment kind of thing. He told her to call if she needed anything while he was gone.

Since he'd be going alone, Bryce wondered if he should fly instead. The idea of driving had more to do with spending time with Deek than anything else, but Bryce reasoned that driving would give him a chance to experience America along the way on the open road.

He packed only the basic necessities and set out. He stopped in New Jersey to fuel up his car.

The only civilized thing about New Jersey is that they pump your gas for you, he thought, as the attendant filled his tank. He wished all states required it.

He drove through Pennsylvania. He was sorry he wouldn't be driving through Amish country. He liked the simplicity of their way of life.

By the time he got to Virginia, he was starting to feel tired. He'd only been on the road about six hours, but he was sick of driving. He booked a room at a hotel in Charlottesville. He took a hot bath and ordered an early dinner with room service. As he ate, he calculated that he had about eighteen hours to go.

He hadn't yet decided what he would do once he got to the ranch. He thought he'd like to tour it, if possible. Maybe he should call ahead and introduce himself to the director. In fact, it would probably be a good idea to arrange a meeting with the director to find out more about how the place was structured. Whatever he was going to establish with his money, he didn't want to go reinventing the wheel. He trusted Cleveland Amory's judgment and would probably design something along similar lines. Just what, he didn't yet know, but he felt sure the idea would come to him as he drove across the nation.

He watched a little local news on TV and rested for a while, but after turning the lights out, he couldn't go to sleep. He wasn't one of those people who couldn't sleep in hotels, he reasoned, so he didn't know why he was so restless. He tried sleeping for another hour or so and then finally turned on the lights and got up. It was just after 11PM. He felt like doing something, but he didn't know what.

He put on some clothes and thought about going down to the hotel bar, but he didn't want to drink. He thought of going outside for a short walk around the hotel to calm his mind, but that didn't seem appealing, either. He wondered if he should take his car and drive into town, but driving was the thing he was supposed to be resting himself from, so he realized that wouldn't make much sense and would just tire him unnecessarily for the next day's leg of the journey.

What if I just keep going? he thought. *I've had a chance to eat and rest.*

The idea excited him, so he packed his things and checked out. He drove off into the night, feeling like a truck driver. He realized that truck drivers get to see a side of America that most others never see, driving through the night along the highway. He smiled when he thought of seeing the sunrise while he was on the road.

Back on the highway, his mood changed, however. It didn't feel quite as exciting as he'd hoped. In fact, it felt a bit scary and desolate. It was terribly dark. He continued on until he got to Tennessee. He was exhausted and wished he were back in his hotel room in bed. He thought about turning around and going back, but he'd already checked out. Besides, it was almost 3AM.

Suddenly, he saw blue and red flashing lights behind him. He thought at first that it was a policeman chasing a speeding motorist, but then he realized he was the only one on that stretch of highway. The police car quickly closed in on him until it was directly behind him. The lights were blinding.

Bryce pulled over, hoping he wouldn't drive into a ditch since he couldn't see at all where he was going. He tried to think why he was being stopped. Maybe a tail-light had gone out. He rolled down his window.

Moments later, an officer came up beside him with a flashlight.

"License and registration," he said shortly.

Bryce fumbled in his glove compartment and handed him the registration, then he took his license out of his wallet. The officer looked at them.

"Stay here," he said. He walked back to his car.

Bryce hoped he'd turn off the lights, but the officer didn't. He tried not to glimpse the reflection of them in the rear-view mirror but it was impossible not to. Those plus the headlights were really blinding. The cool air from the open window felt good, though.

After what seemed like an eternity, the officer returned and handed Bryce his things.

"Do you know you were weaving?" he asked.

Bryce was startled. "No, I didn't."

The officer flashed the flashlight directly in his face. "Have you been drinking tonight?" he asked.

So that's it, Bryce realized. *He thinks I'm drunk.*

"No, officer," he said. "But I am a bit tired. Maybe that's why I was weaving."

"Where are you headed?" he asked.

Bryce felt angry. *Is he allowed to ask that?* he wondered. *It's none of his damn business where I'm headed. Then again, this is the South,* he thought.

"I'm on my way to Texas," Bryce replied.

"Texas?" repeated the officer. "Well, you sure got a ways to go."

"Yes," said Bryce.

"What's a New Yorker like you headed to Texas for?" he asked.

"I'm visiting a ranch," Bryce explained. "The one that was set up by Cleveland Amory."

"Cleveland's that way," said the officer, pointing in the other direction.

"No, Cleveland Amory—a man named Cleveland Amory is the one who set up this ranch," Bryce said.

"Well, we don't want no fatalities along here," the officer said. "I strongly suggest you find a place to get some sleep."

"Yes sir," Bryce said.

The car remained behind him for a few moments and then took off. Bryce was grateful just to be in the dark again. He rolled up the window and realized his hands were shaking. He was tired and the strain of being stopped had shaken him up. He took a few deep breaths to regain his composure. Then he checked his wallet to make sure he'd gotten his driver's license back.

Suddenly, the whole concept of traveling cross-country to the ranch seemed like a terrible idea. What was he going to do there, anyway? If he wanted information about the place, he could call or e-mail. Probably most of what he wanted to know was available to look up online.

He sat trying to figure out what to do, but his brain was in late-night mode, not thinking mode. It wasn't a good time to make important decisions. He reflected for a moment.

If he turned around, he could probably find a hotel; he would check in, sleep, and get back on the road late in the morning. He could drive the rest of the day, take another hotel room, and make it home by the day after tomorrow.

He got back on the highway and took the next exit.

39

When he arrived in New Jersey, Bryce's disappointment had reached its apex. He took stock of his situation. He was stiff from sitting; he'd never been in a car for that long in his life. He'd burned up a lot of gas driving to Tennessee, been stopped by the police, and stayed in three overpriced mediocre hotels. Not only hadn't he reached Cleveland Amory's ranch in Texas, he probably never even needed to go in the first place. And worst of all, instead of seeing America, he'd only seen dirty highways full of big stupid pickup trucks, passenger cars driven by nose-picking morons, and an endless string of nasty fast-food joints.

Bryce pulled into his parking spot in Larchmont with a sense of relief. By the time he was in his apartment, he was tired, cranky, and uneager to catch up on the life he'd temporarily left behind. There were messages on his machine. Claudia had called. Cricket had called. Claudia had called again.

He dialed Claudia's number, hoping to make it a brief hello. He didn't feel like explaining everything to her. She would never understand.

When Claudia picked up, she sounded surprised to hear from him. He told her that he was fine and that he was just checking in. He promised to call her the following day.

"Bryce," she said, "I know now isn't the time, but tomorrow, I think we need to have a talk."

"About what?" he asked.

"Honestly, I don't know what's going on with you," she said.

"There's nothing going on with me. Why do you say that?" he asked testily.

"Three days ago, you e-mailed me and told me you were driving to Texas to visit some non-profit ranch for unwanted animals. You gave me hardly any details, and you didn't answer your phone when I called," she said.

Bryce realized that he'd kept putting off calling her back throughout the trip because he didn't feel like dealing with her.

"It's not even the lack of contact, but just the idea that you'd go off and do something like that with no rhyme or reason," she said. "Married people don't do that."

"But we're not married," he said.

"We're practically married," she said.

"Not any more," he said spontaneously, "Because I'm calling it off." He felt a flush of rage flow through his body. It felt good.

"Bryce," Claudia gasped, "You can't be serious."

"I certainly am. Have a nice life," he said, and hung up.

Well, that's torn it, he thought.

His instantaneous decision would have ramifications that it would take days and dollars to fix, but something felt right about what he had done. For a moment, it felt that even though the world were swirling with chaos around him, he was at the center of the storm, and he was going to be okay.

40

Being newly single meant Bryce had more time on his hands. For starters, he spent Easter alone. Given the breaking of his engagement with Claudia, everyone in his circle was angry with him. He started spending more time with Deek and Tiffany since Deek stuck by him as always and Tiffany was too far down in the social strata to turn her nose up at him.

Deek said Bryce's decision had probably been for the best, and that he should trust his instincts.

Tiffany, on the other hand, told Bryce he was a dick.

"What the hell is wrong with you?" she asked.

Bryce tried to explain that Claudia had begun to suffocate him and that he was reaching out for a new life that she couldn't be part of.

Tiffany shook her head in disgust. "You need to grow up," she said.

Although to Bryce, his problems seemed convoluted and esoteric, to Tiffany, they were extraordinarily simple.

"You don't know what the fuck you want," she said.

"In a way, that's so," Bryce conceded. "My difficulty is that I don't really belong in the class to which I was born."

Tiffany guffawed.

"What's so funny?" he asked.

"You and all these other rich people, you crack me up," she said.

Bryce sighed sharply. "I realize that a lot of rich people are horrible—believe me—but I'm not that kind. I've always wanted to take some of my money and start some kind of a charity with it, maybe something for inner-city kids."

"See? *That's* where you sound like the worst of them," Tiffany said.

"What do you mean?" Bryce asked. "I care. I want to help. If people are cold and hungry, I want to be there to give them soup and blankets."

Tiffany took a long look at Bryce before she spoke. "That's what you people do, you come along and hand out soup and blankets," she said dismissively.

"What's wrong with that?" asked Bryce.

"Because you people never ask why we're cold and hungry in the first place. And the reason we are is because people like you take more than your share of everything," she explained.

Bryce had to admit she had a point. He'd never thought of it that way. He'd sincerely believed that soup kitchens, educational programs, cultural offerings—that these things would surely improve the lives of the unfortunate.

"Take New York," she said. "How long you had soup kitchens there?"

"I don't know," said Bryce. "Probably since at least the eighteen-eighties."

"Are there still people eating at soup kitchens?" she asked.

"Yes, of course," he said.

"That enough proof for you?" she asked, tilting her head to one side.

Everything sounded so obvious the way she said it.

"I told you," Deek interjected. "If she had a Ph.D., she'd be dangerous."

"She's dangerous already," Bryce said. But something about her explanation of the world resonated with him. It made him ask questions he'd never asked before.

"Time to get your ass out of here," she said unceremoniously. "Me and Deek would've went to the movies an hour ago but he was too polite to tell you. I ain't too polite, and I don't want to miss the next showing."

41

Now that the weather was very nice, the three of them decided to take a short getaway together. Deek decided on Newport since he didn't know too many people there who might be put off by Tiffany. He was hoping to break her into his world little by little, starting at the fringes.

They would take Deek's Land Rover since it was roomy. When Bryce met up with them the morning they were to leave, he realized it was the first time he'd seen Tiffany in weather temperate enough to allow for shorts and short-sleeve shirts, because her many tattoos were visible. Bryce wasn't entirely sure if what he could see even constituted all of them; he and Deek didn't talk about things like that, but he rather suspected she had a few in out-of-the-way places as well.

The drive to Rhode Island was picturesque. Tiffany had never been there. She studied the scenery carefully. Someone suggested stopping for lunch.

Bryce laughed. "That reminds me of 'Lunch,' that place in the Hamptons. You've eaten there before, haven't you, Deek?"

"Where? 'Lunch'? Oh yes, I remember that place," Deek said, laughing.

Bryce turned to Tiffany. "It's this little place along the road when you're driving out to the Hamptons, and the only sign you can see at a glance just says 'Lunch,' so that's what everyone calls it. It has a real name—I don't remember what—but everyone calls it 'Lunch.' It's hilarious."

"Oh yeah, 'Lunch,'" Tiffany said. "I go there all the time."

"Oh, do you really?" Bryce asked with pleasant surprise.

"Of course not," Tiffany snapped. "What the fuck would I be doing in the Hamptons?"

Bryce and Deek decided Newport Creamery would be a nice choice for lunch. It was casual enough that it wouldn't intimidate Tiffany but the food was great. They choose a booth. Deek and Tiffany sat across from Bryce.

"What the hell is a 'Awful-Awful'?" she asked, browsing the menu.

"It's a kind of milkshake, Honey," Deek said.

"Then why don't they just call it a milkshake?" she said.

Deek looked at Bryce. It was going to be a long day.

After they'd given their orders, Bryce excused himself to wash up in the men's room. On his way back to the table, he noticed that two very attractive girls were sitting in the booth behind him. They had long platinum blonde hair and one had her sunglasses up on her head. They were beautifully tanned and looked very smartly dressed and well put together. He wondered if he could make an excuse to meet them before they left. He'd think about it while he ate.

He arrived at his seat to witness an ongoing argument between Tiffany and Deek, over the placement of a paper napkin on Tiffany's lap.

"Come on, Tiffany, we've talked about this," Deek pleaded.

"I don't need to do that crap in a place like this," she protested.

"A lady does that everywhere," Deek said.

"I ain't no lady," Tiffany argued.

Ain't that the truth, thought Bryce. Then he had an idea.

"Tiffany," he said, "I think what Deek's trying to say is that the idea of good manners is about behaving in such a way that makes everyone around you comfortable."

"No," Tiffany said. "It's just something rich people use to treat other people like garbage."

Bryce took a deep breath. "Let me tell you a true story. When my sister Susan was eleven and I was nine, my mother threw me a little birthday party at home. Our maid, Margaret, had a son, John, who was about five years old, so Mother told Margaret she could bring John over for the party. We had all sat down and were waiting for Margaret to serve lunch, when John reached over and picked up his finger-bowl and started to drink from it. Susan and I had never seen anyone do anything like that before, so we both started laughing and laughing. We couldn't believe he thought the finger-bowl was for drinking. Then we looked over at Mother, to see if she were laughing too, but she wasn't. Do you know what she was doing? She was drinking out of *her* finger-bowl. That's what etiquette is all about," he concluded.

Tiffany shot Bryce a dirty look. "You're even more of a prick than I thought. Take this," she said, launching a slice of lime at him with one of her utensils.

Bryce was flustered, but he managed to duck. The lime must've hit one of the girls behind him because he heard one of them shout "Hey!"

Laughing, Tiffany then picked up two more lime slices and whipped them overhand, one after the other, at Bryce, but either due to his quick reflexes or her bad aim, they shot past his face. He turned behind him in time to see one of them hit one of the blonde girls in the head.

The girl was furious. She stood up and came to their table, pointing at Tiffany.

"Get that lime-throwing skank out of here," she demanded.

At that, Tiffany loudly barraged her with foul language, leaning forward and yelling across Deek, who was in a state of shock.

Managers and waitstaff came running. The other blonde girl charged in and started screaming about what had happened, pointing at Tiffany.

Ashen-faced, a manager asked them to leave. Bryce and Deek were eager to comply, and they rose from their seats immediately, but Tiffany was just getting started.

She had choice words for the manager, the blonde girls, and a few onlookers at other tables, mostly elderly couples and families with children. Deek finally grabbed her by the arm and pulled her out while Bryce went to hold the door. But before Deek could get her completely through the doorway, she'd managed to get her hands on a rack containing free brochures of some kind, which she violently overturned, spilling papers all over the entrance floor.

"I'm very sorry," Deek said over his shoulder as he and Bryce dragged Tiffany to the car. She kicked them both in the shins and told them to get their hands off her. Passers-by stared in horror. Deek quickly unlocked the car and they all jumped in.

"What's our next stop, The Breakers?" Bryce joked. "Maybe you can topple a few priceless antiques and pee on the rug."

"Shut your mouth," Tiffany warned.

"Stop acting like a feral cat," Bryce shot back.

"Everyone take a deep breath," Deek advised.

"Can you believe those bitches?" Tiffany said, minutes later as they drove along the scenic coast to cool down.

"Sweetheart, I'm not taking their side, but you did throw limes at them," Deek said.

"I was trying to hit Bryce; duh," she explained.

"You shouldn't have been throwing food at all," Bryce admonished. "That's what I was planning to cover in Etiquette Lesson Two."

Deek parked the car where they could see the ocean and they rolled down the windows. Bryce knew Deek had planned to go to the Tennis Hall of Fame during their visit, but after the spectacle with Tiffany, he was sure he'd suggest an early return home.

Two men walked by.

"What's with the guys wearing pink shorts?" Tiffany asked.

"That's not pink," Bryce explained, "It's a color called Nantucket Red. Guys who live in that color do it because they think it makes them seem more cool."

"Looks faggy to me," Tiffany said.

"They're probably not," Deek said. "It's just a fashion thing."

"Yeah, among stupid rich guys," Tiffany added. She looked at her hand and made a small sound. "I broke a nail," she said.

"Do you want me to find a manicurist around here who might be able to fix it?" Deek asked.

"They don't do this kind of nails around here," Tiffany said with a smirk.

"They do all the latest beauty treatments—are you sure you don't want me to try?" Deek asked.

"Nah, I'll just put a bandage on it," she said, digging in her purse. All of a sudden, she looked up and looked at Bryce.

"What is it?" he asked when she didn't speak.

She was silent a moment longer, then she said, "I just had a vision about you."

"Bryce," Deek explained, "Tiffany has this gift, she has visions."

"I've been getting them since I was little," Tiffany said. "Like when I was five, I saw my mom in a car crash and then a week later, she really had one."

"Oh, great," said Bryce.

"And I knew my cousin would meet a dark-haired guy, and she did, and now they live together," she said.

"It's the real thing, I'm telling you," Deek said.

"So what did you see about me?" Bryce asked.

"I saw you in this, like, office building, and I keep getting something about a rose," she said slowly.

"Could it be 'rosebud'? Am I holding a snow-globe in my hand? Does it drop to the floor and roll out of focus?" Bryce said.

"Bryce," Deek said, "She's serious."

"No," Tiffany said, "You're in a—some kind of office, and there's something to do with a rose, and I see you writing," she said.

"Well, I've done a lot of writing before. Do you know what kind of writing?" Bryce asked.

"Don't know," Tiffany said.

"Well," Bryce said expectantly. "Is that all?"

"What else you want?" she asked sharply. "The winning lottery numbers?"

42

Cricket was calling three times a week at this point, and Bryce wasn't answering the phone. He enjoyed listening to her terse messages as she got angrier and angrier that he hadn't responded.

He'd decided that life was too short for dealing with Cricket, and he was never going to speak to her again.

Susan was harder to ignore. When he did finally call her back, she surprised him by telling him that Nathalie had asked her to sound him out to see if he might be willing to give her away at the wedding.

"Nathalie wants me to give her away?" Bryce asked in amazement.

"Yes, you dolt. That's why I've been trying to reach you."

"Well," Bryce thought a moment, "sure, I suppose so. I could do that."

"Good. I'll tell her you'd be open to it. And when she calls," Susan instructed, "pick up the damn phone!"

Bryce sat back in wonder. Nathalie wanted him to take Minty's place. That was something.

43

Two weeks later, Bryce was sitting at the Masterson's eating Polly's tasty shrimp cocktail with Nathalie and Ben. Ingrid had gone to bed early with a headache.

"We're very excited about this," Nathalie said. "I'm making out the final draft of the guest list, and I wanted to ask you if there's anyone you'd like to invite. We'd be happy to add any of your friends."

Bryce thought briefly of Deek, and then of Tiffany.

"No," he said.

"Also," Nathalie said, demurring a little, "Ben had a favor he wants to ask you about."

"A favor?" Bryce asked, looking at Ben. "Absolutely. Anything you want."

"I'm starting a spinoff company of one of my companies and I need a writer, just until we get things off the ground. I don't write well and I don't really know anyone who does, and Nathalie said you used to do a bit of writing," he explained.

"Yes," Bryce said. "I'd be happy to be involved. Anything in particular?"

"Just some general stuff," Ben said, "Maybe looking over the website copy, some of our brochures, things like that. It's all in rough format at the moment, but a writer's touch would definitely improve it."

"Sounds great. When do I start?" Bryce asked.

Ben said, "I'll e-mail you the details."

Later that night, he received Ben's e-mail. It gave the address of an office in the city where he was to meet one of the directors, Ms. Rosemary Rye.

He remembered Tiffany's prediction. Unfortunately, the thing she hadn't told him was whether this situation was going to be good or bad.

Am I going to fall in love with Rosemary and live happily ever after? Or is she going to be a psycho who'll shove me out a window? he wondered.

Later that week, sitting across a desk from her, he was pretty sure she wasn't a psycho. In fact, she seemed very nice. She was about his age, pretty, and somewhat interesting.

She explained that the company was basically an ancillary of Ben's larger company, and that it coordinated charity work. In effect, Ben's company wanted to give back, and this branch was responsible for the giving. He liked the idea immediately, even if he didn't understand all the details.

He was basically told that he wouldn't have to come to the office any more as his work could all be done remotely, save for the occasional meeting.

Considering Tiffany's vision, he thought it might be a good idea for him to get to know Rosemary better. He invited her out for a drink, but she declined, saying she still had a lot of work to finish up.

On the way home, Bryce decided he'd ask Ben for more details about her.

As it turned out, Ben knew very little about Rosemary. He'd had someone else take care of hiring her, and that person had moved on to another company. He vaguely remembered something about her being very accomplished, but that was about it.

During the next month, even though he didn't have to, Bryce often went to the office. Sometimes he saw Rosemary but most of the time she was busy. Ben was certainly getting his money's worth out of her. She was always cordial, though, and seemed pleased with Bryce's work.

44

The days became hot and before he knew it, Nathalie's August wedding was approaching. He panicked a little when he opened the invitation the day it came in the mail. He hadn't thought about whom to bring. He ran through a mental checklist. Nathalie had been his escort on many occasions, but since she was the bride, she wasn't available. Claudia was out since they hadn't spoken since the night he broke up with her and she probably wanted nothing to do with him. Stephanie had separated from Topher, or so he had heard from Susan, and Topher was now living in an apartment and actually working at the rehab as a counselor. Susan had also mentioned that there was a new man in Stephanie's life, a therapist. Bryce wondered if it was the same one that she'd been seeing as a patient.

And then there was Leslie, who was dead. Bryce had thought about her from time to time since her suicide. Once he drove past the bar where he'd sought her after she decided to go on a self-destructive binge, just because he felt the need to reconnect with her somehow. Something in him ached over the tragic manner of her life and death. He hadn't felt it all at once, but over time, as he reflected on her, she seemed a singularly sad case.

Bryce realized he was out of options. There really weren't any other single, available, live women of his acquaintance. Then he remembered Rosemary.

She would probably think it was crazy (possibly even inappropriate) to be asked by him to attend a friend's wedding, but he decided to do it anyway. He caught her after work one evening and, to his amazement, she agreed.

The next day, he walked to the post office and happily mailed his R.S.V.P.

45

The connection wasn't good, or possibly there was a lot of background noise; Bryce couldn't tell which, but in any case, the message came through loud and clear: Rohan was no longer engaged.

He was calling from India and sounded slightly drunk. He was ecstatic. The frog-stomper had shocked and embarrassed his family by getting pregnant with another man's child, and their wedding was called off.

“I don’t have to marry this stupid, cruel, and difficult woman!” he said. “What a blessing!”

“Who’s the other guy?” Bryce asked.

“I don’t know! I don’t care! But I should give him a medal! He’s saved me from a fate worse than death!” Rohan cried.

“It sounds loud there, where are you?” Bryce asked.

“At a party my family is throwing. Don’t tell anyone, but they are even happier than I am, I think,” he said, laughing with joy.

“That’s great news, Rohan, I know how much this must mean to you,” Bryce said.

“And better still, I’m coming back to America next week,” he said. “Maybe I can make a visit to your cabin now.”

“Of course,” Bryce said. “Well, I’ll see you when you get back.”

“Yes—oh, and Bryce,” Rohan said, “I am *so* happy!” Gales of laughter echoed across the planet and into Bryce’s ear. He smiled.

46

When he met Deek and Tiffany the next day, they talked about Rosemary.

“Did anything more come up about your vision?” Bryce asked her.

“No,” she said. “But you want my advice about her?” she asked.

“Yes,” Bryce said eagerly.

“Don’t fuck it up.”

Tiffany and Deek also talked a little about their own upcoming wedding. It had been put off into the future, ostensibly to give Tiffany time to become accustomed to her new position in society.

And, thought Bryce to himself, *to give Deek’s family time to house-train Tiffany.*

Bryce still detested Tiffany’s attitude, behavior, and general rudeness, but he had to admit that she had some winning ways. She was clever and forthright (often shockingly so) and she seemed to care about Deek’s happiness. It would take a lot to bring her into line, but he imagined the finished product being somewhat like Molly Brown.

Deek said his father was coming around to her little by little, and even though Tiffany described her future father-in-law as a “tool,” she was warming to him gradually as well.

“By the way,” she said, turning to Deek, “You know your mother asked me to cover my mouth when I burp? I would’ve did it but I enjoy pissing her off.” She laughed.

Someday this woman would own an island, Bryce realized. Maybe that was the best place for her after all.

47

The writing work was going well and Bryce was enjoying getting to learn about the different charities. He was no stranger to donating money, but he'd never gotten to understand the different venues in detail.

One day, while he was at the office, Rosemary mentioned in passing that they were working on some kind of project for drug addicts. She was saying that she wished they had some kind of liaison who would be familiar with different organizations.

For some reason, Bryce immediately thought of Topher.

"I might know someone," he offered.

It took a bit of wrangling to get his phone number, but Susan had managed to do it; she was amazing at that kind of thing.

"Hi Topher," he said when he called. "Bryce Parnell. How are you?

Topher was glad to hear from him. Bryce was pleased to hear that he sounded good.

Bryce chose his words carefully. "I spoke to Stephanie a while back and she told me that you were in rehab. That's why I'm calling. I hope that's okay."

Topher said his addiction wasn't a secret and that he'd been considering a new career in substance abuse counseling.

"What about consulting?" Bryce asked. "I'm currently doing some work for a company that needs a consultant to help us navigate the charities and assistance programs for people with substance-abuse issues."

Topher said he'd be very interested. He sounded very positive and, thought Bryce, more articulate than he did when they were young.

They arranged to meet for lunch the next day. Topher suggested the same place in Scarsdale where Bryce and Stephanie had broken up, but Bryce instantly said no, mentioning that he knew a really fantastic Greek place in Tarrytown that served saganaki that was not to be missed.

48

Topher and Bryce met at Lefteris, just a few blocks from the Hudson River. Bryce assured Topher the food was sensational.

Sadly, it was a place Bryce had originally heard about from Leslie. Graham had taken her there and dazzled her with flaming cheese. Maybe Bryce could do the same with Topher.

"I've never had flaming cheese before," Topher admitted.

"Few people have," Bryce conceded, "and if you're going to have it, this is the place."

Topher gave a gratuitous explanation of his situation, just to clear the air.

"When we were kids, I never felt like I fit in," he said. "Everyone else was so much smarter than me. I really struggled to keep up. I actually found out last year that I have a learning disorder; that's why everything seemed so much harder for me, but I didn't know it at the time. When I got older, my dad got me a job but I wasn't happy, and I could tell Stephanie wasn't happy with me. Between feeling like an idiot and having a pointless job and a wife I couldn't please, I started feeling pretty low. Then we found out I couldn't father any children, and that was the worst of all. Someone offered me some pills one day, and I just took them. It helped. Over time, that became a regular thing, and then I got into coke. I was just so tired of feeling awful about myself. I don't know if you can understand that, but that's what got me into using substances."

He continued, "Then in rehab, I learned that nothing I could ever use was going to fill up that hole inside me. I had to fill it, because otherwise, the only way I would ever be happy was when I was using, and if I kept using, it was going to kill me. Getting clean was hard, and I failed a lot before I finally got it right—just like everything else in my life, right?" he laughed.

Bryce was speechless. He suddenly felt like the most horrible person in the world. All those years he'd derided Topher, who had been plagued by insecurity and inability. And Bryce could definitely relate to Topher's unhappiness and sense of ineptness. Hearing about Topher's struggle to overcome addiction, he realized he'd misjudged him his whole life. Topher was clearly a good guy. And here Bryce had been sleeping with his wife while he was in a rehab fighting for his life. He felt terrible about what he had done. Topher was still talking, Bryce realized, so he caught the rest of his monologue mid-sentence:

"—and even though things didn't work out, Stephanie has someone new in her life and I'm sincerely happy for her. And as for me, I've got my work at rehab, helping people because I can relate to what they're going through."

"That's amazing," Bryce said. "You have such a healthy perspective on everything."

Topher shrugged. "Something I learned in rehab. You have to have balance in your life."

"But I mean, lots of men would be angry or bitter about their ex-wife seeing someone else," Bryce said.

Topher said "I love Stephanie, and I knew how much she respected her therapist, so when she told me they were seeing each other, I was happy for her happiness."

So it was *her therapist*, Bryce thought.

"What about your future?" Bryce asked.

"I just look at what's in front of me," Topher answered. "I've got a nice little apartment on Garth Road, I love working with the patients in rehab, and I just take time every day to go for a walk or talk with a friend or do something fun just because I feel like it. It's the simple things that make life happy."

They talked about the possibility of Topher doing consultancy for Ben's company and Topher was very agreeable. Bryce agreed to introduce him to Rosemary and she'd be the one to hire him if she thought he was a good fit.

Before they knew it, the most impressive dish of saganaki was placed between them at the table.

"Cheese on fire," Bryce said, picking up a piece of pita bread. "There's nothing quite like it."

49

Apparently, Rosemary was impressed enough with Topher to hire him as a part-time consultant, although after a few weeks, he was offered a full-time position. She explained that eventually, they would have one person to cover each special interest area since they were doing so much outreach to non-profits.

Topher and Bryce had lunch occasionally, and Bryce was surprised to discover that he genuinely liked and respected Topher. Topher was a tremendously caring person, which was a side of him that Bryce had never seen as a kid. Topher could sympathize with anyone, and he explained to Bryce that since he'd been helping people, he realized that this was his true calling. He'd never felt more fulfilled in his life. That he was now becoming successful was simply a by-product of wholeheartedly doing what felt right.

Meanwhile, Bryce still knew almost nothing about Rosemary. It wasn't that she was secretive, but she simply didn't have the kind of personality that lent itself to scrutiny. Bryce had very little information to work with.

She and Topher got on like a house on fire, so he imagined she was a sympathetic person. Rosemary spent a lot of time talking and laughing with Topher in a way she never did with him, which bugged him a little.

One weekend, Bryce invited Topher up to the cabin. He wanted him to have a nice time. He had a feeling that he owed him reparations for the affair with Stephanie, even though he realized Topher probably would say that he understood.

They did a bit of hiking and grilled their dinner outdoors.

"You know, Bryce," Topher said after the meal, "I have a confession."

You've got a confession? thought Bryce. "What's that?" he asked.

Topher said "I always envied you when we were kids. You were so smart and Stephanie liked you so much, and you had this wonderful life."

"Yes, but Stephanie married you," Bryce said.

"Sure, but she never seemed to have a good time with me like she did with you," Topher said.

"Well, I forgive you," Bryce said. "Back then, we didn't know a lot of things that we know now. Speaking of," he said, changing the subject, "just how does a person go about filling that hole inside themselves?"

"Basically, you have to learn to love yourself, and a lot of that happens when you help other people," Topher explained.

"Is that it?" Bryce asked.

"That's it," Topher said.

Somehow, the simplicity of the process didn't surprise Bryce. Great religious figures were always advocating the most basic instructions, like "love each other," "forgive," and "be kind." Bryce was generally disappointed because he wanted something more challenging, perhaps such as levitating, but then he realized that humanity still hadn't really got a handle on those basic precepts, so maybe they were worth repeating after all.

50

Not long afterwards, it was Nathalie's wedding day. Bryce arrived at the Masterson's and had a quick glass of orange juice while he waited for her to come downstairs. Ingrid came down first and said that Nathalie would be finished dressing in a moment. She went to the liquor cabinet and poured a shot of whiskey.

Bryce was surprised; he didn't think it was like Ingrid to indulge in strong drink so early in the day, but she brought the glass to Bryce and encouraged him to have it.

"It's what Minty would have done," she said, handing him the glass. "To steady your arm," she said, winking. Bryce downed the shot.

Nathalie descended the staircase. She looked radiant. Her dress was white and fluffy and around her neck, she wore a jaw-droppingly large ruby pendant which had belonged to Ben's grandmother.

Polly helped get all of Nathalie's dress into the limousine, and then Nathalie and Bryce sped off to the church with Ingrid in the car behind. Bryce had arranged for Rosemary to be picked up and delivered to the church, where he would meet her after he walked Nathalie down the aisle.

It seemed there was very little time for Bryce to say anything, and before he knew it, he and Nathalie had made their way out of the car, up the steps, and into the church. They had a moment in the vestibule before the ceremony started. Bryce raced to collect his thoughts, but the one overwhelming thought was that of Minty.

Somewhere in a semi-skeletal state, Minty was counting on Bryce to give his daughter the send-off she deserved; to be the link between her old life as a single girl and her new life as a married woman. It was an emotional moment to begin with, made all the more poignant by Minty's absence.

"Nathalie," Bryce finally said, "The worst thing about today is that your father isn't here to do this and I'm not a shadow of the man he was, but I knew him well enough to know that he loved you so much that only death could keep him from being here with you right now."

Nathalie's eyes began to well up with tears. He took her hands in his.

"I've got to say what I think he would want you to hear. I know he loved Ben like a son and that he'd be so proud to think of him becoming your husband. And I've known you since you were a child, and you've turned into such a beautiful woman. You'll make the best wife anyone ever had."

Nathalie listened intently, tears streaming down her face.

"You and Ben will have all the joys of marriage and family because you are so loving, and because you are so loved."

Nathalie pressed her damp cheek against Bryce's and he felt her tears in the fabric of the veil. "Thank you," she whispered.

Bryce had a lump in his throat. Now he knew why men cried when they gave their daughters away. He was thankful Ingrid had given him the shot. He swallowed hard while Nathalie dabbed at her eyes, then she smiled and stood beside him. She took his arm and they walked to the sanctuary doors. The music began, and they processed towards the altar.

Bryce stared straight ahead but he could feel the eyes of everyone upon him. He made a quick sidelong glance to see if Nathalie was okay and realized he was walking beside a young queen. Her bearing was solid; she was every bit Ingrid's daughter. He stood taller as they continued on. In the space of a few steps, as he paraded past faces he'd known since boyhood, he thought of Nathalie laughing and eating ice cream, Nathalie begging for his sweater when she got cold in the cinema, Nathalie playing Scrabble on an autumn evening. She was his good friend, and always would be, he realized.

They were nearing the front of the church. Bryce saw Susan, who looked deeply moved, and Patty, who was awash in tears. Rosemary sat with them and she smiled at Bryce. Bryce saw Ingrid, who looked proud, and he was pleased.

They had reached their destination, and the priest began the ceremony.

"Who gives this woman to be married to this man?" he asked.

"I do," said Bryce. Nathalie leaned over and kissed him lightly on the cheek, then turned and stood beside Ben. Bryce stood staring after her until he heard a faint *"Psssst!"*

It was Susan, motioning for him to take his place in the pew. He was still standing in the aisle like an idiot.

51

The wedding was beautiful and Bryce realized Rosemary looked lovely. She always looked nice at work, but she looked especially pretty today, all dressed up.

After the ceremony, the two of them rode to the reception in a car with Susan and Patty. He could tell they approved of Rosemary.

At the reception, they had a wonderful time, and whenever Bryce walked past a group, he heard people murmuring "He's a neighbor of theirs," or "The family thinks very highly of him." It was in that context it occurred to him why Nathalie had asked him to give her away. She'd done it to restore his reputation, which had all but been destroyed after he broke his engagement with Claudia. She knew everyone knew and loved Minty and would be very anxious to see who she'd decide would fill his place. There were relatives of Ingrid's who could've done it, or Aris Jorgensen, or even Uncle Clement. All would've been much better options than Bryce, but she chose him because she loved him and wished him well. On the most important day of her life, she was thinking of what she could do for him. The realization touched Bryce profoundly.

He and Rosemary had a lot of fun dancing. During one of the orchestra's breaks, Aunt Fluff came over to greet them.

"Rye," she mused. "What an interesting surname."

"It's English," Rosemary said. "My father's from Liverpool, but my mother is half Irish and half Indian."

The orchestra began playing again. Bryce grabbed Rosemary's hand and pulled her to the dance floor. "Excuse us, Aunt Fluff," he called behind him.

"You're eager for another dance," Rosemary said.

"I just figured this would be more fun than hearing ethnic commentary from Aunt Fluff," Bryce said. "I had no idea you had such a fascinating background."

"Don't we all?" she said.

52

By late September, Bryce had made the cabin his primary residence. He and Rosemary had been seeing each other since Nathalie's wedding. A non-profit Bryce was forming on his own was still in its infancy, while Susan and Patty had started the process of adopting a baby.

In the early afternoon, Bryce and Rosemary drove to Freund's Farm Market and carefully curated baskets of fresh vegetables. They had guests coming for the weekend.

That evening, Bryce sat by the fire and looked at the faces glowing in the golden light: Deek and Tiffany, Rohan, Topher, Nathalie and Ben, and Rosemary.

Outside, the massive trees that had sheltered his family for generations stood tall. Inside, there was happiness and love.

Bryce sighed, and was at peace.

THE END

About the Author

Born in Manhattan and raised in Texas, Cinzi Lavin is an award-winning writer-composer known for her "Nantasket Trilogy" of musical dramas about the seaside town of Hull, Massachusetts. She has professional experience as an actress, singer, instrumentalist, and educator, and her career highlights include a performance by invitation at the White House. She and her husband make their home in Litchfield County, Connecticut.

www.ingramcontent.com/pod-product-compliance
Lightning Source LLC
LaVergne TN
LVHW091009080826
845145LV00003B/1189

9781736635001